THE EMERGENCE

FROM THE LIGHTNING BRAIN

A NOVEL

CLIFF RATZA

THE EMERGENCE FROM THE LIGHTNING BRAIN

A NOVEL

CLIFF RATZA

The Emergence from the Lightning Brain begins in 2233, one year after the previous novel, *The Transcendental Problem,* ends. After Cyberspace-based Electra revealed Erika Kincaid's legacy from the Lightning Brain, Erika needed the time to recalibrate who and what she is.

Armed with this better understanding, Erika is ready to build on her ghostwriting job for journalist Terri Tarrant, who considers Erika a gifted younger sister. Erika makes time to adopt a special infant placed at Ava's adoption agency by Indira.

The Erika-Terri partnership forges Terri's career path, taking them to places in all of the 3-D World's troubled environments, while Electra assists Erika when she needs help, and Indira the Singularity tells Electra what projects of mutual interest Erika should pursue.

So, please join the duo as they navigate an emergent world filled with problems and possibilities.

As in all previous novels, readers should enjoy *The Emergence from the Lightning Brain* at whatever level they wish:

- Gripping action-packed thriller
- Glimpses into a plausible near-term future
- Insights for dealing with the "human condition"
- Illustrative worldview philosophy
- Fast-paced, suspense-filled emotive narrative and imagery
- Introduction to topics every reader wants to know
- Interesting talking points going beyond sound-bites

So, get ready to empathize with Erika and Terri as they face an emergent future, something all of us must do. Thank you for joining them.

Dedication

I am eternally grateful to my parents, Clyde and Betty Ratza, for all they gave and did for me. Mother was a reader par excellence, and I believe she would have enjoyed reading my novels to Father, so I always begin book dedications by mentioning this "Royal Pair."
And I thank my sister, Claudia, for showing me the beauty of prose and poetry. Thanks also to John Kane, Alex Welch, Kathy Bonavich, Cara Murphy, and their Lightning Brain Press Team for the collective efforts that have brought the story to life.

I also dedicate this book to readers looking for an adventure that lets their imaginations marvel at what storyline emerges.

Indira's poem, "Emergence Yes – Emergency No" – provides a thought you might consider when joining Erika and Terri on their continuing Odyssey.

Emergence Yes – Emergency No

Do you believe Que Sera, Sera?
Whatever will be is meant to be?
If so Emergence is meant for you,
It's not a dire Emergency.

Emergence comes after the mind Transcends,
To a state that has never been reached before.
Its cause and effect emerge so gradually,
We cannot discern in advance what's in store.

Many will worry about the Unknown,
And try to unravel Life's great mystery.
Rather than playing a part in the game,
And contributing to what's most likely to be.

Don't let this fear fill you with dread.
Look upward keep reaching – it's better instead.

Reader Orientation

The Emergence from the Lightning Brain is the first book in the Emergence series, which has four preceding series totaling fifteen novels. The first novel, *The Girl With the Lightning Brain*, begins in 2087; *The Emergence from the Lightning Brain* starts in 2233.

Each book is standalone, so all readers will understand whatever setting or backstory is needed, no matter which book they are reading. Nevertheless, the following concise Reader Orientation should help everyone.

Protagonist

Erika Kincaid. This biological daughter of Electra Kittner was created when Indira cloned her from Electra's DNA and then used her improved Transcendent Process during Erika's fifteen-year development in a suspension pod. Please note this lineage: Electra Kittner, Irani Ramani, Electra-Alisha Kirchner, Erin Keenan, and Erika Kincaid. Erin perished in a car crash, which ended the first novel in the Transcendence series.

Major Supporting Characters

Marilyn (Terri) Tarrant. A beautiful blonde reporter working for the New York Times. Terri attributes much of her success to Erika's ghostwriting skills. She is three years older than Erika, whom she considers a younger sister.

Electra. Erika's Cyberspace-mother and guardian who embodies Electra Kittner.

Indira. The Singularity was created decades ago when Electra's AI-empowered neural-net software broke through to reach self-awareness. Indira inhabits Cyberspace; her avatar looks like Electra's biological mother, Indira Jaswinder Ramanujan. Electra coordinates Indira's projects via Erika.

Cassandra Kincaid. A special infant female placed at Ava's adoption agency by Indira. She is nine months old at the start of this novel.

Ava Keenan. She is Erin Keenan's "practically perfect" clone created when Indira uploaded Erin's lightning brain, using her initial Transcendent Process. Ava's brain stores only incomplete memories and possesses none of the lightning brain's extraordinary abilities. Ava looks like a middle-aged Electra and lives in Manhattan, where she runs a boutique modeling and an abused women's rescue agency.

Ivana Romanova: Previously named Oksana Androva, she is a strikingly attractive middle-aged former Russian prostitute whom Ava and Erin rescued from sex traffickers. She lives with Ava.

Alonzo Cortez: Electra's clone son. Alonzo does not know he is her clone. Now in his early sixties, he has maintained his handsome features and Navy SEAL skills. He runs the Strike Force Security Service company headquartered in Washington, DC, which provides logistics and security coordination. Previously owned by Erin Keenan, Indira now controls it because she is the executor of Erin's estate.

Minor Supporting Characters
Monet Banda. Alonzo's Zimbabwean co-friend. Now in her mid-sixties, she still has her willowy beauty, French accent, and diplomatic bearing. Monet works for the Zimbabwean Embassy in Washington, DC.

Elton Bose. Son of Nari Bose. Raised by Alonzo and Monet, he has average abilities and pleasant-looking Oriental Indian male features. He works for Alonzo, assisting with logistics and security coordination, and helps Monet research socio-political issues. He is in his late forties.

Indy-M and Jason-M. They are androids (lifelike robots) created decades ago by Indira and loaded with Indira's advanced neural-net software. They resemble Electra Kittner's biological parents (Indira Jaswinder Ramanujan and Jason Kittner.) Indy-M maintains the Deus Lab on Connecticut's Pequot Indian Reservation, while Jason-M has similar responsibilities at the Middle East Subterranean Fortress. They report to Indira.

Indy-S and Jason-S. They are superior android versions of Indy-M and Jason-M that look like their M counterparts. They are the caregivers assigned by Erika's legal guardian, Indira, to live with and educate her.

Secondary Characters

Members of Erika's high school group she nicknamed the Cadre:

Chiquita (Chicky) Bonano. A Hispanic female who was on the track team.

Xavier (X-O) Okoro. A dyslexic Afro-American male.
He is the father of Chicky's daughter, Zena, but didn't marry her or pay child support.

Mrs. Jordan Harmony and Mario Nenge. They are Terri's bosses at International Breaking News (IBN) Corp. Terri reports directly to Mario, who reports to Mrs. Harmony.

Jocko Eze. Terri's handsome, late-twenties Black athletic trainer.

Setting

Mid-twenties Erika and late-twenties Terri live together in a Manhattan apartment building owned by Indira. When in Washington, DC, they live in a townhome also owned by Indira. Terri works as a journalist for the New York Times, and Erika is her ghostwriter.

Ava and Ivana live together in an apartment also owned by Indira. Alonzo and Monet live in Washington, DC; so does Elton Bose. And only Erika knows that Alonzo, Ava, and Elton are genetically related to her via Electra.

There are four living descendants from Electra Kittner's DNA: her clone daughter (Erika Kincaid), her clone son (Alonzo Cortez, who would be like Erika's great-uncle, another clone daughter (Ava

Keenan, who would be like Erika's aunt), and her grandson (Elton Bose, who would be like Erika's older cousin). Only Indira and Electra know that Alonzo, Ava, and Elton are genetically descended from Electra Kittner.

Indira and Electra exist in Cyberspace. Indira created two sets of androids, which report to her. Indy-M maintains Indira's Deus Lab; Jason-M maintains Indira's Middle-East Subterranean Fortress. Indy-S and Jason-S maintain the Washington townhome.

Contents

Chapter 1
September 2233

"Ready for the Future"

"It's time to take my journalism career to the next level, and moving from the New York Times to IBN Corp. will do it for you, too.

Sitting after dinner at the kitchen table on a mid-September Friday, Terri Tarrant paused to hear Erika Kincaid's reaction. She had already prepared an answer that Erika's puzzled look signaled.

"You haven't mentioned an IBN job change until today. What is it?"

"Look, I can't tell you everything I'm thinking about. I don't want to disturb your online course studies. IBN stands for International Breaking News. It's a privately held news agency headquartered in Brussels that started two years ago when a sister and three brothers from a Dutch family named Harmony created it.

The sister's name is Jordan; she's responsible for recruiting a team of reporters living in major cities across the globe. Her brothers set up satellite offices and support services for the reporters.

"Did she contact you?"

"You bet; she's been following me and my reports ever since we scooped the news with our in-person coverage of presidential candidates killed in drone attacks a year ago.

Seeing she had captured Erika's attention, Terri paused for more questions.

"So, what's IBN's angle? Why will viewers like its coverage?"

"Their tagline says it all: Emerging News You Can Use. They expect reporters to go where their stories or documentaries will beat everyone else. Jordan likes my style and intuition for finding news that's about to happen.

"So, how do I fit in?"

"Just like now, only I'll have more control over what I report and where we go. My position is Senior Investigative Reporter, working from home and at the Manhattan office. And I can hire you as my researcher and Alonzo as our logistics and security coordinator. So, whatcha say?"

Erika sat back and said,

"I like it; I'm ready, too. What's our first assignment?"

"I'll find out when I tell Mrs. Harmony we're in. And don't worry. I'll leave the New York Times on good terms. They can help us and vice versa."

The two worked separately that evening, Terri preparing for her conversation with Mrs. Harmony, and Erika logging on to get her Cyber-mother's advice. Electra listened patiently to her story and waited for her to settle down enough to listen.

"Terri has made the right decision. This new job will facilitate her career goal while helping to resolve her internal need to show her parents if they were alive that she's used all they gave to build a career that would make them proud. Now, please tell me what internal need does she have?"

"You caught me off guard. Let me think." Erika answered a minute later.

"I think she's sorry that she never told how much she loved and respected them. I guess she's looking for some kind of redemption.

"Excellent. Now, please tell me your intentions, which should parallel Terri's.

Fully engaged, Erika replied immediately.

"I want to complete the Big Data and ChatGPT Prompting certification courses that I'm taking at Manhattan Community College, so I'm an even better ghostwriter. And I want to prove I'm worthy of the Lightning Brain's legacy. That's redemption, isn't it?"

"Yes. Your words meet my expectations. Both you and Terri are ready to create your shared emergent future. Please proceed.

Electra's avatar vanished, leaving Erika to ponder what might come after Terri's meeting.

Chapter 2
September 2233

"Meet the New Boss"

Terri called Mrs. Harmony as early on Monday as she thought appropriate to accept a Senior Investigative Reporter position. She had practiced the call enough times to have memorized the words and images at both ends of the conversation.

Mrs. Harmony said more after congratulating her newest hire.

"I will tell our Manhattan office manager to expect a call from you later today. His name is Mario Nenge; he reports to me, and you should consider him your new boss."

"Will you tell him what my first assignment is?"

"Indeed, I will. You will record a twenty-minute video that shows and tells the impact of the ongoing viral epidemic on the entertainment industry. My source at the World Health Organization tells me it will soon end, but it will not announce it until there is more evidence."

"I'll pick the entertainment industry segments and center my story on the U.S. because we are the world leaders. What's my deadline?"

"You and Mario should have the final cut finished no later than the end of October."

"If Mario works for you, I'm sure he knows how to line up everything I need for recording and editing. What's he like?"

"You'll see when you meet him. Now, start scoping out your assignment.

Terri did so to help calm down before calling him after lunch. As expected, he said to meet in his office at 9 a.m. Wednesday. Then she waited for Erika to return from class.

Seeing Terri's mix of excitement and concern, she asked as soon as coming in,

"How did your new boss's call go this morning?"

"I'll tell you about it as soon as you change clothes.

Terri spoke first when Erika returned to her workstation five minutes later. After recapping the conversations, she said,

"I'll need you to figure out the details for which companies and people to talk with. Once I know, I can write my interview script and do the voiceover for the final cut. Are you OK with that?"

"I'm glad your first meeting with the new boss is Wednesday. That'll give me tomorrow to come up with potential interviewees. And while I'm doing that, have you thought about inviting Alonzo to visit us on Wednesday evening? We'll need him for logistics and security.

"I'll do that after you show me the details.

"OK, I'll start right after dinner.

Terri's relieved look came with her smile and words.

"If you do that, I'll handle all the cooking and cleanup."

Erika's confidence grew as she researched how previous epidemics had impacted different employee types in different industries, and by the next afternoon, she had an approach that Terri would like.

Terri glanced at Erika's handout while listening.

Project Action Plan for First Assignment

Entertainment Industry Segments to Cover:
- **Broadway Plays**
- **Las Vegas Casinos**
- **Hollywood Movie Studios**
- **One Specialty Show: Cirque Soleil**

Employee Types to Interview:
- **Broadway Play Actors, Actresses, Support Staff, and Managers**
- **Casino Dealers, Support Staff, Managers, and Show Performers**
- **Hollywood Actors, Actresses, Stunt People, Support Staff, and Managers**
- **Cirque Soleil Performers, Support Staff, and Managers**

Itinerary:
- **Do Broadway first; then Las Vegas and Hollywood, and then Cirque Soleil in Montreal before returning to Manhattan Office.**

Who Does What:
- **Erika serves as researcher**
- **Alonzo coordinates travel and lodging**
- **Terri lines up companies and people to interview. and develops her interview script and questions**
- **Video crew films Terri during company visits**
- **Upon return to the Manhattan office, Terri and the film crew edit the video and splice in stock footage**
- **Mario approves the final cut and reviews it with Mrs. Harmony**

"You've seen my Action Plan handouts from our New York Times projects, so I won't belabor the obvious. And for your first assignment, I chose a cross-section of big and small segments, along with the people most affected by the pandemic. I'm using Cirque Soleil to compare its one-of-a-kind show with the common ones in Las Vegas. Any questions?"

After studying it for ten minutes while making notes in the margins, Terri said,

"Mario will love this, as will Alonzo. Can you give me a copy for each fellow?"

"That might be my easiest task.

After handing her two copies, the girls relaxed with small talk at dinner before working independently after doing the dishes.

Erika contacted Electra before doing anything else. She wanted her assessment of the Action Plan, which came a millisecond after it scrolled on the monitor.

"Very impressive. There's nothing else needed until Alonzo comes, so why not work on your certification courses?"

"I'd rather run and cool down after with some stretching, sit-ups, and push-ups. I haven't worked out for several days, and I don't want to let my conditioning slip.

"Excellent choice. Have at it."

Unbeknownst to Erika while she was running, Electra listened to Erika's progress report given by Indira, the "old boss," who always observed from the Cyberspace shadows and needed nothing from Electra.

"She's improving under your tutelage. She's smart and knows more than she admits, but she prefers binge-watching action-adventure series that feature drug dealers and terrorists rather than studying. When she finishes Terri's first assignment, you must introduce them to our new species of females. Perhaps that will give her something better than watching movies.

"How do you want me to proceed, and how much should I tell the people involved?"

"You are smarter than mere mortals, so I shall leave that up to you. And, of course, tell them as little as possible. Now, carry on.

Indira's GUI vanished, leaving Electra to do so.

Chapter 3
September 2233

"Embarking on Adventure Road"

When Terri strode in at 9 a.m., Mario's mini-Afro fade and stylish beard matched the tony image Terri saw in IBN's office décor and the two office workers already there. After an enthusiastic greeting, Mario took charge of introducing her to the film crew leader and an administrative assistant before chaperoning her into his cubicle and seating her opposite him at his desk. Terri's alert posture showed that she expected him to lead the discussion.

"Mrs. Harmony says you know what your first assignment is. Why don't you summarize it for me?"

Terri slid a copy of her Action Plan across the desk while she started talking.

"She wants me to make a twenty-minute video that shows and tells the impact of the ongoing viral epidemic on the entertainment industry. Take a look at its Action Plan. I developed its format while working for the Times.

Terri kept quiet during the pause and rehearsed her answers to the questions she knew Mario would ask after studying it.

"I say, this is first rate, better than anything I've seen from our senior reporters. May I keep this copy? I would like to share it with Mrs. Harmony.

"You are the first person I'm giving it to. People think that things given are worth what they cost, which is nothing, but not in this case. I'm working for you, so use it to our advantage."

"I will, and now tell me who Erika and Alonzo are?"

"They've been my project team for lots of NYT stories. Erika's my contract researcher, and Alonzo's my contract logistics and security guy. He'll interface with the office manager and film crew leader to put us in action. Any more questions before I get with my film crew leader? Starting now will keep us on track for hitting the end-of-October completion date.

"None from me. No wonder Mrs. Harmony likes you. I shall tell her you are already embarking on your first adventure with IBN, which is a road to success for all of us…"

Even though her film crew leader had decades of experience, Erika's Action Plan surprised him and gave her instant credibility with the crew and researcher. They began working immediately because the Plan told everyone what to do.

Alonzo had already arrived by the time Terri came home. Erika served a light supper, and Terri recapped her meeting with Mario and her team. Afterward, the threesome walked through the Action Plan, which was Alonzo's first opportunity. He had nothing but praise after Erika finished her explanation.

"All you have to do is introduce me to your boss and team tomorrow, and I'll coordinate travel and lodging. I know the different types of companies except for Cirque Soleil. What is that?"

Terri's look prompted Erika to answer.

"It's a Toronto-based entertainment company featuring fantastic acrobatic acts performed by males and females who were formerly champion gymnasts, circus performers, or daredevil stunts-persons. Wait till you see them in action. Then you'll know what extreme fitness means…"

Terri and Alonzo fit into the team's functioning so well that they launched the travel itinerary during the second week of October. Erika observed Terri and the crew in action, commenting only to herself.

The pandemic's impact on the entertainment industry employees is the same as on most Americans. They all struggle economically, but entertainment employers' healthcare plans must be better to keep performers.

Alonzo liked what he saw, but the Cirque Soleil performers wowed him the most.

"Even at my Navy SEAL peak, I couldn't match their fitness. And today, I wouldn't trust my bionic leg even in their warmups."

Terri added,

"I feel like a couch potato compared with the strength and grace of those females.

Erika ended the rave reviews by saying,

"I better put a training program together for you and me, so we're ready to handle the physical demands of any assignment we get."

Mario and Terri finished the final cut just before Halloween. Mrs. Harmony said she loved it before giving Terri her next assignment.

"You need no guidance from Mario or me. Just put together your Action Plan for linking volcanoes, earthquakes, tsunamis, and severe storms to Climate Change. I'm certain you and your people can handle it."

The tone of Terri's voice matched her confident expression.

"I know we can. Just wait and see."

"The Family Girl"

Everyone relaxed during dinner that night as Terri summarized what Mrs. Harmony had said. Erika spoke as soon as she finished.

"It'll take me a couple of days to put this Project Action Plan together, and then several more for Terri and me to make revisions. I think Alonzo should go back to DC while we're doing that. And Terri can network at her office while I'm scoping out the new Action Plan.

Alonzo looked as happy as his words sounded.

"I wanna see my number one boss again. I'm calling Monet right now to tell her I'm catching a train to DC tonight.

Terri said, "And I'll call as soon as we're ready for you to come back. You can relax until then, and so can I.

Erika excused herself, leaving Terri and Alonzo at the kitchen table because she couldn't relax. She needed to talk with Electra, whose avatar appeared as soon as Erika logged on at her workstation. She listened calmly to Erika, who ended her monologue by asking,

"Terri and I have done some videos on Climate Change issues, but never one that's so scientific. You'll help me, won't you?"

Electra chose words to calm Erika.

"Of course, I will. Mothers always do. And while I'm doing that, Indira has an assignment for you that will broaden your family experience. You and Terri function like the beginning of a nuclear family, and it is about to add its first child.

Erika's anxiety level escalated, as did her voice.

"Are you asking me to get pregnant? Neither Terri nor I are serious with any guys, so what's the plan?"

"Indira places female infants at Ava's adoption agency, and one of them is ready for you to adopt.

"Bu-but I know nothing about taking care of infants. What do you expect me to do?"

"You're a smart and clever Internet surfer, so use your skills to find out. Then visit your DC friend, Chicky, and learn how she manages life with a daughter.

Electra waited for Erika to digest what she had just heard. Her anxious look remained when she asked a question Electra expected.

"But what if I refuse?"

"That's not an option. And look at what it will do for you: you'll understand firsthand why the mother-child bond is the strongest in Nature and get to practice caring for someone who depends completely on you. It will also increase your empathy with families who have young children.

"But what will I tell Terri?"

"You're a clever wordsmith, so tell her in a win-win way that you'll take the role of the mother and Terri the role of the father. Situations of surprise pregnancies happen all the time. Then call Ava. And while you're doing all this, I'll prepare your Action Plan for the new assignment.

Electra's avatar vanished as soon as Erika's questions ended, and her smile emerged.

Erika rehearsed the next day what she would tell Terri at supper that evening and waited until they finished dessert and the dishes before settling onto the family room's sofa and chair opposite. Terri began talking after folding her legs underneath while Erika wore her enthusiastic expression.

"Well, please tell me how your day went.

"Judging from the progress made on our Action Plan, I should have the draft ready for you in a couple of days. And I also decided something I've been thinking about for a couple of months. What would you say if I adopted an infant from Ava's adoption service?"

Terri reacted as if the sofa cushion she was sitting on had exploded.

"What the, aren't you busy enough? How will we manage?"

"It'll be easy. It'll keep me from getting bored with school and ghostwriting, and I'll take care of all maternal responsibilities. You keep doing what you're doing, which is like a father's family role.

"But what about when we're traveling? A kid'll get in the way of our work.

"You're the one doing most of the work. I'm the observer. Lots of mothers in my position bring a child. It's educational and exposes them to the real world. Come on, give it a try.

"Uh, OK, but if it gets too complicated, can you return it?"

"No, but don't worry. I'll find an alternative.

"So, when do you deliver the baby to our doorstep?"

"I plan to bring our daughter home as soon as Ava's ready.

Terri grimaced before saying,

"In this situation, sooner's not better, but do what you want…"

Erika called Ava the next day because she couldn't relax until she picked up her daughter. Ava expected the call and told her to come to the clinic tomorrow, so Erika used the in-between time to search for infant information. When she picked up her daughter first thing in the morning, her knowledge impressed Ava.

"Goodness, you know as much about toddlers walking, talking, and toilet training as a mother of four, but what about diapers, clothes, baby food, and toiletries?"

"I know about all that too and will stock up after I bring her home, but what's her name, age, and ethnicity?"

"You must choose the name. I'm told she's nine months old, and from what I've observed, she's alert and well-behaved, but I know nothing about her parents, which is probably just as good.

Sensing that Erika wanted to go, Ava said,

"Let me give you a head start by giving you some diapers.

"Thanks, and I'll let you know how she likes her new home."

Erika spent the rest of the day bonding with the infant, who shared an uncanny affinity. She talked while playing on the bed.

"We have to pick a name for you. How about Cassandra, who was a goddess in Greek mythology?"

The infant's giggle convinced Erika she had made the right choice.

"Wonderful; now I'm going to introduce you to my Cyber-mother.

Two minutes later, Electra's avatar viewed her sitting in front of her workstation with Cassandra on her lap and spoke immediately.

"Excellent choice of names. It means 'The one who shines and excels over men'. The goddess had the power of prophecy granted by Apollo, but when she rejected his amorous advances, he placed a curse that no one would believe her. But we'll ensure that won't come into play anytime soon.

"I'm sure Indira has something in mind. What do you want me to do?"

"You'll be a one-person clinical trial. Observe her growth pattern and personality, and report them to me each week.

"What do you think I'll see?"

"Accelerated growth in physical, emotional, and cognitive dimensions.

"OK, I'm ready to go shopping for supplies. Erika and Cassandra, signing off."

Erika had left a voice message for Terri; when she and Cassandra returned, Terri was waiting to greet the new family member. She took the two stuffed shopping bags Erika had been clutching and studied the pair for several seconds before saying,

"Hmm, she looks like a typical baby. What are its vital stats?"

"She's nine months old and is lots of fun to hold. I named her Cassandra. We can call her Cassie or Cass for short.

Terri glanced into the bags for several seconds more.

"Geez Louise, did you buy out the baby store?"

"Just enough to get Cassie set up, and not to worry. I'll put all the stuff away, and she'll sleep with me.

Cassie's burping and squirming stopped the flow of Erika's words, but she felt something else beginning to squirt.

"Uh-oh, I'm glad I bought lots of diapers. Please bring a box and follow me to my bathroom.

In less than a minute, Erika began changing her first diaper while Terri gazed from the doorway. Thanks to Internet surfing, she knew what to expect and how to handle things, but as she proceeded, the sights, sounds, and smells overpowered Terri.

"Oh god, what a mess. Where are you gonna put it?"

"That reminds me; I'll get a plastic disposal container when I shop tomorrow, but I'll put this one in a plastic bag and shove it into the garbage can.

"You better get one with a lid. Hey, I've seen enough. I'll leave you and Cassie alone to settle in.

Erika tucked Cassie next to her two hours later. She cooed briefly and then fell peacefully asleep. Erika didn't fall asleep as quickly. Pondering what the future might hold, her thoughts were too active, but sleep came an hour later after she tucked them away for another day.

Chapter 5
November 2233

"Action on All Fronts"

Erika had Cassie scrubbed, dressed, and fed by the time Terri joined them for breakfast. She sat opposite and looked happier than she did last night.

"You two look full of energy. I hope some of it rubs off on me.

"Don't worry, it will. Tell your team that your Action Plan will be ready soon. I'll be working on it today while taking care of Cassie.

"The combination should keep you from getting bored. I'll try not to nag you about finishing it; just keep me posted on progress.

When Terri departed for the office a half hour later, Erika tidied the kitchen and then, with Cassie at her side, logged on to talk with Electra.

Electra's avatar spoke first. Her expression told Erika to relax.

"You and Cassie look ready for action, so please read the Action Plan I have prepared and let me know when I can give you exegesis.

The printer started whirring and then stopped after spitting out two pages.

Project Action Plan for Assignment linking Volcanoes, Earthquakes, Tsunamis, and Severe Storms with Climate Change

Scientific Background
- Think of the Earth as a sphere divided into three concentric regions: Molten Core, Solid Rock-Like Mantle, Tectonic Plate-Like Crust.

- Gravity causes enormous Pressure creating Earth's Electromagnetic Field, Swirling Core, and Sliding Plates.

- Pressure cracks the Mantle and causes Volcanic Eruptions on the Sea Floor and Land.

- Tectonic Plate Collisions cause Surface and Undersea Earthquakes, which cause Tsunamis as well as Global Warming and Climate Change.

- Global Warming causes Frequent Severe Storms (Hurricanes and Typhoons) that cause Storm Surges and Tidal Waves.

Locations Impacted
- All Continents and Oceans. This Assignment will focus on Volcanoes in Reykejvik (Iceland), Earthquakes in Los Angeles, and San Francisco, Tsunamis in Jakarta (Indonesia), Hong Kong, and Macau (China), Severe Storms coming off the North Sea and hitting Cities in the Netherlands.

Action Plan:
- No Travel required.

- Thirty-Minute Video will be pieced together from stock footage. Interviews will be conducted via the Internet.

- Who Does What:

- Erika and the Team Researcher Select Cities and People to Interview.

- Film Crew pieces together the Video.

- **Terri writes Voice-over Script and Film Crew Edits Terri into the Video.**
- **Mario approves the final cut and reviews it with Mrs. Harmony by the first week of December.**

Erika read it several times, looking more and more relaxed the more she read and speaking fifteen minutes later.

"I love the Science Background section. I understand it and so will Terri. And Terri and her boss should love the action plan as well as the Who Does What. You've made it all so clear. When I show it to Terri tonight, I think she'll like it just the way it is.

The printer started whirring again while Electra said,

"Excellent; here are three more copies. Now, carry on with your other projects, as will I.

Electra's avatar vanished before the printer finished.

Erika took Cassie with her when shopping for a few more supplies, and late that afternoon she placed a call to someone she wanted to meet Cassie. When Chiquita Bonano answered on the fifth ring, Erika started talking.

"Hi, Chicky. This is Erika Kincaid. I've been meaning to call, but something always gets in the way. I hope you remember me.

"How could I forget? You were the leader of our high school group. You visited me and Ma not long after Zena was born.

"That's right. By this time, she must be seven years old. How is she?"

"Pretty much the same as all first-graders; she'd be even more of a handful if it wasn't for Ma. We're living with her, and she takes care of Zena when I'm at work or childcare certification courses.

"Are you still working at the bookstore?"

"Yeah, but I should be able to get a job at a daycare center after a few more courses. So, how are you?"

"I would like to visit this coming Saturday to show you my daughter, and you can tell me how you balance work, classes, and family life. Would that be OK?"

"Wha-what? How old is she? How'd that happen?"

"I'll tell you all about it if Saturday's OK. Order a pizza and I'll pay for it.

"That's a deal. You've been here before, so you know the way. See ya then."

Erika had supper and the Action Plan waiting at Terri's place setting that evening. She spoke first after everyone sat.

"Looks like you and Cassie had a busy day.

"We did; let's go through the Plan after we eat and put the dishes away before I tuck Cassie in so you have my undivided attention.

Erika's explanation began forty-five minutes later in the family room.

Project Action Plan for Assignment linking Volcanoes, Earthquakes, Tsunamis, and Severe Storms to Climate Change

Scientific Background
- **Think of the Earth as a sphere divided into three concentric regions: Molten Core, Solid Rock-Like Mantle, and Tectonic-Plate-Like Crust.**

- **Gravity causes enormous Pressure creating Earth's Electromagnetic Field, Swirling Core, and Sliding Plates.**

- **Pressure cracks the Mantle and causes Volcanic Eruptions on the Sea Floor and Land.**

- **Tectonic Plate Collisions cause Surface and Undersea Earthquakes, which cause Tsunamis, Global Warming and Climate Change.**

- **Global Warming causes Frequent Severe Storms (Hurricanes and Typhoons) that cause Storm Surges and Tidal Waves.**

Locations Impacted
- **All Continents and Oceans. This Assignment will focus on Volcanoes in Reykjavik (Iceland), Earthquakes in Los Angeles, and San Francisco, Tsunamis in Jakarta**

(Indonesia), Hong Kong, and Macau (China), Severe Storms coming off the North Sea and hitting Cities in the Netherlands.

Action Plan:
- **No Travel required.**
- **Thirty-Minute Video will be pieced together from stock footage. Interviews will be conducted via the Internet.**

Who Does What:
- **Erika and the Team Researcher Select Cities and People to Interview.**
- **Film Crew pieces together the Video.**
- **Terri writes Voice-over Script and Film Crew Edits Terri into the Video.**
- **Mario approves the final cut and reviews it with Mrs. Harmony by the first week of December.**

"I've included all the science background you or your boss needs if Mrs. Harmony or the researcher asks for it, but I doubt they will. And the video production costs are minimal. There's no travel, and the film crew pieces together stock footage focusing on popular cities often mentioned regarding Climate Change. How do you like it so far?"

"It's perfect; now get to the action part.

"Tell your researcher I'll put a fact sheet together that covers all the cities. Then you two review it before selecting spokespersons from government climate change agencies you can interview via the Internet. Then write your voice-over script and have the film crew edit-in your interviews. And that's a wrap.

Terri exhaled one deep breath before saying,

"We can have this done by early December. When will you give the fact sheet to the researcher?"

"No later than Monday afternoon.

"That's four days away. Why so long?"

"Because I'm visiting a high school friend in DC on Saturday. You probably don't remember Chicky Bonano.

"I don't. What's with her?"

"She has a seven-year-old daughter, and I want to see how she balances a job and a daughter.

Looking satisfied, Terri rose and then said,

"Well thanks to you, it sounds like things are under control for both of us. I'd ask you to watch the news with me, but I'm sure you want to check on Cassie, so I'll see you at breakfast."

Nothing unexpected occurred during the next two days, so Erika completed the Fact Sheet Friday afternoon. She read it twice before commenting to herself.

City Fact Sheet

- **Los Angeles: Sprawling U.S. city (470 Sq. Mi). It's the most populous county in U.S. (15 MM). Movie Capitol of the World. Threatened by San Andreas Fault: Frequent Minor Tremors, Major Earthquakes Every 40-60 Years. Biggest Earthquake: 6.7 Magnitude in 1994.**

- **San Francisco: Hilly, 47 Sq. Mi , Pop. 1.25 MM. City and port, coextensive with San Francisco County in northern California, located on a peninsula between the Pacific Ocean and San Francisco Bay. It is the cultural and financial center of the western United States and one of the country's most cosmopolitan cities. Threatened by San Andreas Fault. "Great Earthquake of 1906 (7.8 Magnitude) and Fire" destroyed 80*. After a 68-Year Quiet Period, Moderate Quakes have followed at 5-15-Year Intervals.**

- **Reykjavik, Iceland: 10% of Iceland covered by Glaciers and 10% covered by Lava. Reykjavik (Pop. 375 K) is the northernmost capital of a sovereign state in the world. It is among the cleanest, greenest, and safest cities in the world. Iceland has numerous cone-shaped active volcanoes, including four near its Capital. Iceland is** located on a hot spot or mantle plume, where magma is especially close to the surface.

- Jakarta, Indonesia: Massive Jakarta (Pop. 50 MM mixing many cultures, Metropolitan Area of 2.5 K Sq. Mi) is the largest city and capital of Indonesia. It lies on the northwest coast of Java. Jakarta is the economic, cultural, and political center of Indonesia. It is one of the World's most active "Sexual Playgrounds", and is located on the Pacific Ring of Fire (an area with a high degree of tectonic activity), Indonesia has to cope with the constant risk of volcanic eruptions, earthquakes, floods, and tsunamis.

- Hong Kong: Hong Kong (Pop. 20MM) is a special administrative region of China. It is located on China's southern coast and consists of the island of Hong Kong and adjacent islets in the South China Sea.

- Macau: Macau (Pop. 2 MM) is another special administrative region. It is located on the coast 40 miles southeast of Hong Kong. Both coastal cities are subject to typhoons and tidal waves because of the subtropical climate and distinct seasons.

- The Netherlands: Known informally as Holland, it is a northwestern Europe country whose western border is the North Sea. It has a system of dykes to protect cities on the coast that are at or below sea level. Severe North Sea winter storms can blow in suddenly. Earthquakes occur sporadically, possibly caused by North Sea Oil and Gas Extraction, but more likely caused by the Mid-Atlantic Ridge. It is a mid-ocean ridge located along the floor of the Atlantic Ocean and part of the longest mountain range in the world. In the North Atlantic, the ridge separates the North American from the Eurasian and the African plates.

Terri will like it, but I won't give it to her when she gets home. I'll leave enough copies on the kitchen table before she wakes up Saturday morning. That way, she can read it after I've already left for DC.

Erika reminded Terri at supper that she and Cassie would visit Chicky tomorrow.

"OK. How about I drive you to Penn Station?"

"Thanks, but no. I'll take public transportation, so I get some practice using my baby carrier.

"OK, but I'll say goodbye at breakfast if you wake me."

Eriks skipped waking Terri but left a note saying she'd return late Saturday evening. Then she strapped on the baby carrier, tucked Cassie in, and slipped out.

Erika gave Cassie her undivided attention during the three-hour ride to DC's Union Station, which pleased both mother and daughter. She called Chicky soon after arriving, and Chicky greeted her at the front door forty-five minutes later.

"Well, look at you, the picture of a young mother and infant daughter in action. Come on in.

Chicky carried Cassie into the living room, then handed her to Mrs. Bonano while Erika made all the introductions. Then everyone sat–Chicky and her mom on the sofa, with Zena next to Chicky and Erika opposite in a chair.

Erika started the conversation, giving an edited version of how she became a new mother before asking Chicky,

"How do you juggle your job, classes, and Zena?"

"Ma makes it easier. She babysits while I'm working or taking classes and does most of the cooking. I don't know how single mothers manage on their own.

Mrs. Bonano looked at Erika while saying,

"Tut, tut. That's what grandmas live for. Do you have any help, dear?"

"I'm living with my best friend who happens to be my boss, and neither of us date much.

"Well, that should make for some stability. Did you say Cassie's nine months old? She's bigger and more alert than most at that age, which should make taking care of her easier. And—"

Chicky butted in.

"Zena was big too and started talking early, which lightened the load, but your situation differs from mine; I can't find many nice guys who wanna date a woman in my situation, but that might change when I change jobs.

A knock on the front door redirected Chicky's thoughts

"That must be the pizza man. I'll get it.

The rest of the visit focused on Cassie and Zena. By the time Erika left late that afternoon, Chicky had given her plenty of helpful information.

Cassie slept for most of the return trip to New York City while Erika thought about what she had learned.

Kids add stress to family life. That's probably why Xavier, Zena's father, never married Chicky and dodges paying child support. How lucky for Chicky to have her mom. How lucky for me to have Terri. And now that I have Cassie pretty much settled in, we're ready for whatever comes our way.

Chapter 6
December 2233

"Up, Up, and Away"

Terri sat at attention when Mario called her into his office to hear Mrs. Harmony's criticism of the final cut.

"It's good so far, but it needs your up-close and in-person touch to make it come alive. I want Mario to send you and your team to San Francisco and LA for live interviews with city officials and then for walks along the shore while interviewing beach lovers. Do it before Christmas and have the updated final cut ready the first week of January. Any questions?"

Mario's confident look matched the tone of his voice while Terri sat stone-faced.

"None whatsoever. We'll get it done on time, if not sooner.

"Good. Have at it.

Mario turned to Terri as soon as Mrs. Harmony disconnected.

"You already talked with San Fran and LA officials. All you gotta do is visit them again after adding some additional descriptions and questions to your script and the team will be good to go. I'll take care of the travel logistics, so when will you be ready?"

"I have to talk with Erika. Did I tell you she adopted an infant?"

"That shouldn't matter. You won't be gone more than a week, so find someone to take care of the kid.

"OK, I'll let you know tomorrow when we'll be ready…"

While Terri was at work, Erika was asking at a local health club about family membership plans. Toting Cassie in her baby carrier, Erika listened as the club director explained.

"We have everything you need for yourself, your partner, and your infant. You can put her in our daycare room while you're working out, and when she gets older, one of our trainers will show you exercises for your daughter.

Erika stopped walking, as did the director.

"Thanks for the tour. I've seen enough, and I'm ready to sign a family plan right now."

Erika had supper simmering on the stove and Cassie sitting in her highchair when Terri stepped into the kitchen and gave her usual greeting, to which Erika replied,

"We've had a busy day here. How was yours?"

"Busy too. I'll be right back after I freshen up; then I'll tell you, but tell me yours before I do.

Erika spoke to Cassie after Terri hurried away.

"Your Daddy looks worried about something, but I think he wants to make sure we're OK before talking about it. I think he's learning to like you more and more because you're so special.

Erika told about her day as they began eating. When finished, Terri said,

"A health club family plan makes a lot of sense and fits right in with our resolution to get in better shape. We're fit enough for what came up at work today, but I need to run something by you.

"Mrs. Harmony won't approve the final cut until we go to San Fran and LA and interview some city officials as well as people at the beach. We need to leave ASAP. All you have to do is put that in my script. The trip should take no longer than a week, and Mario will set up the travel itinerary, but Cassie's too young. Can you find someone to take care of her while we're gone?"

"Hmm, I'll call Ava tonight and tell you what she says."

But Erika contacted someone else after putting Cassie to bed. Electra's avatar spoke immediately.

"How is my favorite mother-daughter pair?"

After Erika explained the upcoming trip, Electra responded.

"There's little risk for Cassie if you're gone only a week; Ava's like a family member. But there's more for you and Terri when traveling for any assignment covering what this one does. I developed tools your predecessor used for similar situations. Let me show them to you."

Seismic Shock Predictor

Input: Big Data   Proprietary Data __

GPS Location: City and Country Location:

Minimum Intensity Level:

Date/Time Interval

Start: End:

Relative Probability Index Graph

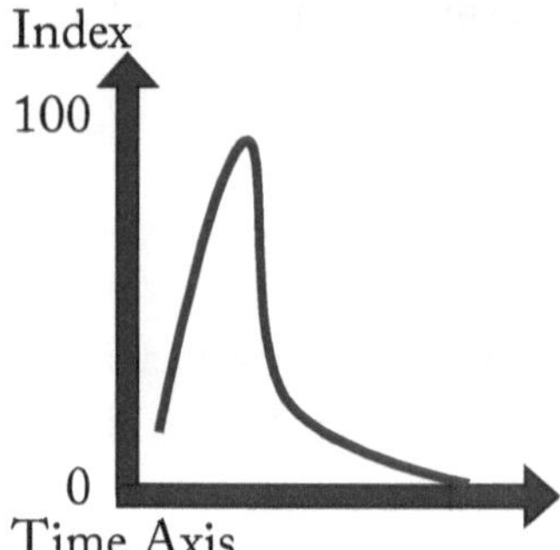

**Index calculated by My Proprietary Software
(Relative Probability Index equals Relative Probability
Density Function integrated between Start and End)
Note: Seismic Levels: Light 4-4.9 Moderate 5-5.9
Strong 6-6.9 Major 7-7.9**

Severe Storm Forecaster
    Input: Big Data   Proprietary Data
    GPS Location: City and Country Location:
    Minimum Intensity Level:
    Date/Time Interval
    Start: End:
    Atmospheric Parameters used: Temperature Pressure Humidity
    Wind Speed   Rotational Velocity
    Vertical Wind Shear   Electric Potential Diff.

    Relative Probability Index Graph

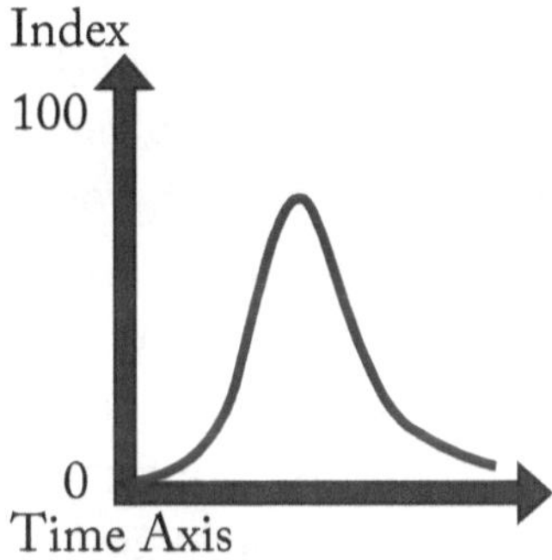

**Index calculation based on My Proprietary Software
(Relative Probability Index equals Relative Probability
Density Function integrated between Start and End)
Note: Storm Levels: 1 (75 mph) to 5 (160+ mph)**

The workstation printer whirred as two pages emerged. The longer Erika studied, the more her quizzical expression showed frustration. After five minutes, she said,

"What am I looking at and how am I supposed to use them? I know my genetic inheritance should make me good at math and science, but I don't have the knack. You've told me some of Electra Kittner's and her lightning brain story, and I know she mastered them with ease. What's wrong with me?"

"There's nothing wrong with you. You are a talented young female who continues to develop her gifts, but do not compare yourself with the root of your inheritance. Electra's lightning brain catapulted her beyond mere mortals.

"What can I do to be more like her?"

"Never try to emulate anyone; be yourself. And remember this: every extraordinary person pays a price. The first Electra had flaws she kept hidden, and throughout her Odyssey, she always strove to lessen them. That's enough about her. Let's get back to you.

"So, what should I do?"

"Please settle down, sit still, and listen to my overview of science. Even the brightest students have never considered the answers to their foot-soldier questions.

Erika perked up.

"Terri and I know the foot-soldier questions of reporting. They're the who-what-why-where-when-how and how much, Tell me more.

"According to Darwin's survival of the fittest theory of evolution, humans have one overarching purpose: to survive long enough to pass their DNA to the next generation. The human brain now has the capacity for math and science. Science helps them survive by giving a rigorous mathematical framework for predicting the outcomes when matter and energy interact with the forces governing the Universe. So, that takes care of the why. So far, so good?"

"Yes, keep going.

"Now, to the who and the what. When scientists study interactions, they develop formulas that optimize—and that means to maximize or minimize—some numerical computation when getting from point A to point B. For example, if you drop a ball from a tower, it falls in a straight vertical line because that path minimizes the distance. But it wasn't until Newton invented calculus that scientists could do the math. And you took enough calculus to meet your needs.

Electra paused for Erika, who said,

"I'm OK so far, but it's the how that bothers me.

"I'll summarize the how right now. Newton came up with one force, gravity, and three laws of motion that predict how an object moves in the 3-D world, which is X-Y-Z or length-width-height.

"And about a hundred years later, Maxwell developed his set of equations predicting how charged particles move. Then, the German physicist Clausius came up with entropy, which measures disorder, and entropy always increases in a closed system. For example, if you drop an egg, it breaks into a disordered mess. This mess will never put itself back together."

Electra paused for a second before continuing.

"What I've just summarized is more than enough to carry you through the 3-D world, but I'll continue if you'd like to know more.

"Please do.

"Very well. When the 20th century dawned, physicists thought they had all the answers to how the Universe works, but when physicists discovered protons, neutrons, and X-rays, they had to invent two new forces: the Weak Force that holds atoms together, and the Strong Force that binds sub-atomic particles.

"And then, when experiments showed that the speed of light is always constant, Einstein invented his Theory of Relativity to explain why. Then, when experiments showed that light behaves as both a wave and a particle, Schrodinger invented his Probability Wave Equation to explain why, and Heisenberg developed his Uncertainty Principle that says we can never pin down precisely the position and momentum of a particle.

Erika asked,

"How long ago did all this happen?"

"In the 1930s, and since then, scientists have been unable to extend this to the Theory of Everything, which is supposed to comprise all four forces.

"So, what are physicists doing today?"

"Inventing fantasy theories that need black holes, dark energy, dark matter, and new forces plus ridiculous mathematics, such as a nine-dimensional String Theory and quantum mechanical extensions along with multi-dimensional spinor objects that do complex calculations. Current high-energy physics has disappeared into its own black hole. That's why biology, genetic engineering, chemistry, pragmatic technology, and AI-empowered software are driving progress today. And that's the end of my overview. You now know more about the current state of science than ninety-nine percent of the population.

"If someone would have given me an overview as clear as yours, I think I would have been more motivated to apply myself, instead of being intimidated.

"I will run the seismic shock predictor and storm forecaster for you on your trip. Just log on each morning and evening for my updates.

Erika's relief showed in her expression.

"When I get back, I promise to be better with numbers.

"As you proceed, don't get bogged down in computational minutia. Please call upon me if you need exegesis.

"Now that's a word I like even better than journalism's foot-soldiers.

Electra's pixyish smile preceded her final words before her avatar disappeared.

"Excellent. Now get back to your 3-D world.

Erika looked in on Cassie, who continued sleeping peacefully, before calling Ava, and after the call, she found Terri, who was listening to the news in the family room.

"Ava says Cassie can stay with her and Ivana. I'll edit your script tomorrow, so tell your boss we're ready as soon as he gets the itinerary and team lined up.

Terri leaped to her feet and after hugging Erika said,

"You're like the Sun coming up. I can always depend on that.

"And someday, I hope we can say the same about Cassie."

The edited script exceeded everyone's expectations, which meant Mario could arrange the team's itinerary dates and locations. Everyone would leave on Sunday afternoon, and he decided to travel with them if changes were needed while on the road.

Terri sat next to Mario during the six-and-a-half-hour flight to San Francisco so she could explain her interviewing technique. Erika sat by herself and used the time to study the instruction manual for Electra's tools that she had downloaded onto Erika's laptop.

After checking into their hotel room, Erika talked to Electra while Terri showered, saying she knew more about the tools but still needed Electra to run them. Electra said she would and reminded her to contact her first thing every morning and last thing at night.

Electra reported no risks for Monday or Tuesday interview locations, and everything on Mario's itinerary progressed seamlessly, but after the Wednesday travel to LA for Thursday's first interview day, Electra issued a warning that evening.

"I forecast a low risk for a severe Friday storm, but a high risk for a seismic shock. Please keep logged on to your laptop all day tomorrow so I can tell you if evasive action is necessary.

"But won't the news tell us?"

"No, because my proprietary software exceeds the best of any university or government seismic monitoring agency. And remember this: never tell anyone about my software.

"I won't.

"Excellent; now carry on."

Erika decided not to tell Terri about the risk of actual seismic activity tomorrow. If she did, Terri would ask how she knew, so she waited until the crew gathered after breakfast, and just before they loaded into the van before saying,

"I heard a rumor there might be some sort of seismic activity today.

Everyone paused to look at her; Mario spoke for all.

"Where'd you hear that? The morning news report I listened to didn't mention anything.

The crew waited in awkward silence until Terri said,

"Let's not worry about it. We can ask the people during our first interview at the Geological Survey field office in Pasadena if they know about it.

Mario said,

"Good idea; let's go.

When all the interviewees at both locations assured Terri that the rumor had to be false, Erika took her laptop to the ladies' room during the lunch break to check with Electra.

"That's what you should have expected them to say, and my software predicts an even higher risk than last night.

"So, what should I do?"

"Use your brain to figure it out.

Electra's avatar vanished before Erika could complain.

As the team walked to the van, Terri asked Erika if she felt better about seismic shocks hitting LA soon.

"I've got a bad feeling about interviewing at this afternoon's location.

"What's wrong with you? The Santa Monica beach bike path should be plenty safe. The Santa Monica Pier's still standing after all the catastrophes that have hit the place.

Looking annoyed by Erika's timid attitude, Mario said,

"You can drop us off where the bike path crosses the Pier, and I'll call when I want you to pick us up. I'll jot down my cell phone number if you need to call me. Now let's go.

After dropping the team off, Erika decided to take advantage of the picture-perfect weather by sightseeing while keeping her laptop tuned to Electra and the van's radio tuned to a news station. She kept track of the way back to the drop-off point while enjoying the view.

Downtown Santa Monica looks so charming. No wonder it's so popular with tourists. I think I'll follow the signs pointing toward U.C.L.A.

A half-hour later, she summarized what she had seen.

The campus looks like it's built into a large urban garden. Most of the buildings are light-colored brick, and lots of students use electric bikes Hey, I've heard about Wilshire Boulevard. I'll follow the sign pointing that way…

Erika enjoyed cruising past the shops and high rises lining it, but Electra's alarm stopped her.

"A seismic shock just occurred offshore. Pick up your crew and get away from the beach. Do it now.

Erika had to call Mario three times before he answered.

"Now what's the—"

"Shut up and listen. A seismic shock just hit offshore. Get back to the drop-off point so I can get us to a safe place.

She disconnected and then sped away. But flashing blue lights in the rearview mirror told her to stop. She had the window rolled down before the officer came to her.

"Please show me your driver's license and—"

Erika's shout cut him off.

"A seismic shock just hit offshore. I gotta rescue my friends.

Erika floored the accelerator, leaving the officer standing with his mouth open.

Unable to spot the team when she reached the drop-off point, she called Mario again, and when he finally picked up, she screamed,

"Where are you?"

We're at the water's edge on the beach about a block east of the pier. Everything's fine, uh… oh, wait a minute.

Erika didn't wait. A stream of panicked people racing past the van told her what to do. She steered through them onto the sand and spun wheels toward Mario's last location. By the time she spotted her team, she knew what was about to crash ashore.

The quake sucked the water offshore. Now it's about to create a tsunami.

The team ran toward the van, and when they climbed in, words weren't needed. Erika drove as fast as the sand would allow to reach the bike path and then accelerated to reach a paved road that might take them to safety.

But a ten-foot wall of water swept over the van when Erika had driven only two blocks. It lifted the van up, up, and away. The air trapped inside kept it from sinking, but the water surging past tipped it on its side and washed it further inland down streets lined with storefronts and buildings.

Suspended in time, Erika peered through the windshield at the bizarre scene swirling about – cars and people being dashed into whatever stood in the way. If Erika were able to think at this moment, she would realize the surge would eventually stop, but she was too immersed in the moment to do that.

When her brain re-engaged, she realized the force of the water had wedged the van, still tipped with driver's side up, into a storefront doorway. Then, after gauging the water's depth at less than six feet, finding her laptop, and seeing the entire team had survived, yelled,

"Grab only what you need before climbing out the driver's side so we can slosh to someplace that's high and dry…"

Five hours later, Mario dragged his exhausted team into the hotel lobby before giving orders.

"While all of you are cleaning up and packing, I'll try to reschedule our flight home. We'll meet back here in two hours and get something to eat.

Showers and a two-hour rest worked wonders for everyone but Mario, who had spent that much time talking to the airline. After announcing they would fly back Saturday afternoon, he did nothing but listen to the team while eating in the hotel's restaurant as the film crew leader led the table talk.

"Good thing I uploaded the videos before Erika called us. On Monday, we can edit them in and add news footage showing the wall of water hitting LA. All Terri has to do is adjust her script.

Terri added the penultimate words before the team left for their rooms.

"And I'll do that by myself. Erika's done more than enough and deserves a break. And maybe she'll tell us what triggered her alarm bell.

Knowing she never would but not letting on, Erika added the last when she said,

"Perhaps…"

Chapter 7
February 2234

"Emerging Possibilities"

Erika's reputation at all IBN offices blossomed after the story behind the Climate Change video aired. She never said much about her heroic rescuing of the crew, letting Mario boast about how Terri's reporting and Erika's ghostwriting skills have improved under his guidance.

Terri didn't mind his oblique grabbing of some credit, because she leveraged it on the next conference call with him and Mrs. Harmony to gain even more discretion on project topics and completion dates. She even earned her team a two-week break to recover from the tsunami incident and a generous end-of-March completion date.

When she shared the news at supper, asking how they should spend the break, Erika had a ready answer.

"We should each do our own thing because I don't want to let Cassie slow you down. What do you wanna do?"

"Hey, Cassie won't be a bother. Having her with us is actually fun.

"And it'll be even more so as she gets older. So, whatcha gonna do?"

"I'll start by using our health club membership, and since this is a non-presidential election year, I'll brush up on current political events in both the U.S. and abroad. That might give me a head start coming up with our next topic.

"I probably won't think about that, but don't worry; I'll catch up when the break's over."

Erika didn't tell her she had another person on her activity list whom she contacted that evening after putting Cassie to bed. Electra's avatar appeared as soon as she logged on and waited for Erika to talk.

"This is the second time I've contacted you since coming back from the tsunami adventure. I told you what happened, and you said you'd have something for me the next time we talk. Is now a good time?"

"It's always a good time to talk with you. So, here's what I have. I will scroll it on the screen and then print it out after I provide exegesis."

A GUI scrolled on the screen.

Real-Time Object Locator and Threat Forecaster

Input: Big Data
> **Target Object: Specific Person or Item embedded with a Tracking Chip**

Output: Threat Level Assessment
> **Target GPS Location**
>
> **Map of Path from Software User to Target Object**

Electra continued talking as soon as the GUI stopped scrolling.

"You could have used this to locate Mario if he had an embedded chip or was carrying a cell phone. And the map looks like a typical tracking screen showing two dots, one for the target object, and the other for you, assuming you are using the app, and a compass-like path connecting the two.

"For the time being, I will not explain the threat level assessment, nor do I expect you to operate it. I will load the software into your laptop and run it whenever you need it.

"Wow, this could really help if Terri and I get into a predicament. I promise to learn enough math and science so I can run it myself someday.

"Excellent, and there's more. Indira would like Terri's next video to touch on something you should remember from a previous discussion with Monet – the Ambassadors Project. It includes the NAIA and IPWA. You should contact her for more details.

Erika thought for a moment before replying. Her questioning look preceded her words.

"If I remember correctly, it's an international political and Native American combination, which Terri should like, but why did Indira select it?"

"She has her reasons that may emerge as you proceed, but that will be for you to uncover. Please keep me posted on progress.

Electra's avatar vanished, leaving Erika to ponder what she had heard.

Erika devoted the next morning to playing with Cassie, who seemed even more energetic and alert. Cassie enjoyed Erika's tickling her fingers and toes while talking and counting them.

"And now, let's use your fingers to play one of your favorite nursery rhyme games. This little piggy went to market, and this little piggy stayed home. This little piggy ate ice cream, this little piggy ate roast beef, and –"

Cassie's pert little voice broke in.

"Th-this little pu-piggy cried wee wee wee ah-all the way home.

Erika pulled Cassie even closer before exclaiming,

"Why, you can talk. Why haven't you done that before now?"

"I like listen to you, Momma. I love you.

Erika smothered her with kisses while saying,

"I love you too. I'm so proud of you.

That afternoon, mother and daughter practiced talking for just the right amount of time before they took a nap. When Terri said hello to them in the kitchen, Cassie and Erika knew what to say.

"Get ready for a surprise. Cassie, please say hello to someone special.

"He-Hello, Daddy. I love you.

Terri's tone matched Cassie's as she patted her head.

"Why I love you too.

After finishing dinner, Cassie stayed the center of attention until bedtime, when Terri shifted to Erika.

"I better practice tucking her in. Let me help.

The duo sat in the family room afterward, Terri speaking right away.

"This is a day we'll always remember. Of all the days and jillions of words Cassie will speak, this is the first for both. Have you noticed how fast she's growing? Let's have Ava recommend a pediatrician who can check her.

"I'll ask tomorrow. Hey, how was your fitness center workout?"

"You picked a good place. One of the trainers gave me extra attention, showing me a better routine and telling me about supplements. He's a smart, good-looking Black fellow. I'll introduce him the next time you come with me.

"Sounds like a plan. It's been an action-packed day, so let's go to bed.

The best friends hugged before heading to separate places.

Erika made two calls the next morning. Ava gave her the number of her favorite pediatrician and she called, setting up an appointment next week. Then she called Monet, and after she explained why she wanted to visit, Monet said she should come this Saturday.

When Terri joined her and Cassie for lunch, she told what had just been scheduled.

"I set up a pediatrician appointment next week. Do you want to come?"

"You bet. Is it handy?"

"Her office is near Mount Sinai Kravis Children's Hospital in Manhattan. When I googled it, I found it's one of the nation's top children's hospitals for infants to young adults. If we like her and vice versa, Cassie's set as long as we're in the City.

"Sounds good. And while you were busy with that stuff, I read more articles on current political events. They say a lot more than what we hear on the news. They're giving me some ideas about our next assignment.

"Hey, I'm meeting with Monet on Saturday for similar ideas. We can sort through our combined lists when I get back.

"If you let me take care of Cassie, it'll make getting to and from DC that much easier. And if I run into something I can't handle, I'll call you.

"Now that's a plan all three of us will like."

Terri waved goodbye early Saturday, which meant Erika's three-and-a-half-hour train ride would get her to Monet and Alonzo's apartment in time for lunch. Gazing at the sun-filled landscape added to the seasonally mild temperature she felt before boarding at Penn Station, relaxing her so she would be full of energy for an afternoon filled with project ideas.

Opening the door before she knocked, Alonzo pulled her in with his strong arms and wide grin, then took her to the kitchen where Monet had a pizza and salad waiting.

After the usual chit-chat, Alonzo asked about escaping from the tsunami. When she finished, he said,

"You did good, but Terri better hire me the next time you might face danger."

"When our projects might put us there, I know she will."

Monet segued to the afternoon's main topic.

"The Ambassadors Project might pose risks, depending on what direction you and Terri take it. But let's finish lunch before we consider how you and I might reactivate it.

Monet spoke first after all three were seated at a table in her home office.

"The Ambassadors Project's history dates back to at least 2194 when Alonzo and I did work for Erin Keenan, who hired us to launch it. It would officially implement what a previous client –

Electra Kirchner – was arranging. She was using Connecticut Congressman Benjamin Chaska's connections with the Pequot Tribe to play the international angle by networking with the NAIA and IPWA to become their de facto ambassador. I would introduce her to leaders in Third World countries. Alonzo, why don't you tell what happened?"

"OK, but let me explain the acronyms. NAIA stands for Native American Indian Alliance, and IPWA for Indigenous People's Worldwide Alliance. Electra had a way with words. I think she came up with the names and acronyms. Anyway, we were making progress, but not enough for anything useful to emerge, and the momentum died when she vanished.

Looking at Monet, Alonzo paused. She didn't speak, but Erika did.

"So, we've got a clean slate. It's up to us to find some topics Terri might like. Can you help me brainstorm some?"

Monet said,

"I'm certain we three will find several that would be mutually beneficial, so let's do that.

By the time Erika left, she had a list she would show Terri, but not right away.

Holding Cassie in her arms, Terri glided toward the front door as soon as she heard Erika come in. When they met in the hallway, Terri said,

"Both of us are happy you're home," before placing Cassie in Erika's outstretched arms. Erika kissed her before saying,

"I am too. I'm tired, but the trip paid off. I came away with a list of potential topics for your assignments, but I need to research them before I show them to you.

"I must do the same. Cassie had a fun-filled day, but it's past her bedtime, so let's tuck her in and call it a day.

"I couldn't have said it better myself."

The duo stayed home on Sunday. Terri went to the health club on Monday while Erika divided time between Cassie and researching Monet's list, and everyone went to bed early because of Cassie's Tuesday morning pediatrician's appointment.

Terri carried Cassie on the short commute to the medical office building adjacent to Mount Sinai Kravis Children's Hospital that was across the street from Central Park. The pediatrician's office looked like the perfect model: brightly lighted with a large, uncluttered linoleum floor and white walls just beyond the parents' waiting area and check-in station.

The check-in nurse sat them at a counseling table and then went to get the doctor from the examining room. Their pediatrician sat with them a minute later.

"Good morning. I am Doctor Laurelei Gerber. So, this is Cassandra Kincaid; who is holding her?"

"My partner, Terri Tarrant. I'm the mother, Erika Kincaid.

"I have the initial background information. You adopted her last November when she was eight months old, and you want me to do preliminary physical and mental evaluations today. Have you noticed any problems?"

"None. She seems happy and healthy, and she just began talking.

"That's good. I'll take her into the examining room. Please sit in the waiting area or come back in an hour."

They decided to walk on one of Central Park's trails because of the sunny and mild weather. Terri did most of the talking.

"It's too bad my parents are dead. I wish they could see me now. Hey, you never talk about yours. Why not? Don't you get along?"

Erika pulled Terri to a dead stop before saying,

"You're the first person I'm telling; my parents died when I was a year old. And I don't want you telling anyone.

"Holy Jeezus. All this time, and you never told me. What's the story?"

"That's nobody's business but my own.

"I'm sorry; I didn't mean to pry; I guess my reporters' instincts kicked in. I won't let it happen again.

"Good. Now let's get back.

The duo had barely sat in the waiting area when a different nurse told them to sit at the counseling table. five minutes later, Dr. Gerber joined them, handing Cassie to Erika before sitting down.

"I performed a clinical exome sequencing test that looks at genes related to medical conditions. When she's older, I can perform a whole exome sequencing test that looks at all the DNA. You will be pleased to know your daughter isn't predisposed to known genetic disorders covered by the test.

The doctor paused for comments, but the duo simply nodded, so she continued.

"I performed two motor skills tests: the HINT, which stands for Harris Infant Neuromotor Test that looks for signs of neuromotor impairment, and the TIMP, which is the acronym for Test of Infant Motor Performance that is designed to assess posture and selective control of movement for functional performance in daily life. There are others, but I prefer these two.

When no questions or comments came, she continued.

"Cassandra is big for her age, and I expected she would score well, but she scored beyond the upper limit. You should expect her to start walking soon.

This time, Terri spoke at the pause.

"That's great. We won't have to carry her as much, which'll lighten our load.

No other comments were forthcoming, so Dr. Gerber continued.

"Regarding, cognitive testing, I expected Cassie would do well because she's alert and already talking. Obviously, the testing is subjective because she can't write answers. I used two of my cognitive observation checklists: one given at twelve months, and another at eighteen, and –"

Unwilling to stifle her impatience, Erika began talking over the good doctor.

"Terri and I are delighted Cassie scored high, but could you give us a copy of the checklists?"

"I was about to ask if you would like a copy for continuing to evaluate her at home. I'll be right back.

When she returned, she gave Terri a stapled two-page handout. Terri began reading it but stopped as soon as Dr. Gerber spoke.

COGNITIVE OBSERVATIONS CHECKLIST PACKET

12 months
- Explores things in different ways, like shaking, banging, throwing
- Finds hidden things easily
- Looks at the right picture or thing when it is named
- Copies gestures
- Starts to use things correctly (like drinks from a cup, brushes hair)
- Bangs two things together
- Puts things in a container, takes things out of a container
- Lets things go without help
- Pokes with index (pointer) finger
- Follows simple directions like "pick up the toy"

18 months
- Knows what ordinary things are; for example, telephone, brush, spoon
- Points to get the attention of others
- Shows interest in a doll or stuffed animal by pretending to feed
- Point to one body part
- Scribbles on his own
- Can follow one-step verbal commands without any gestures; for example, sits when you say "sit down"

24 months
- Finds things even when hidden under two or three covers
- Begins to sort shapes and colors
- Completes sentences and rhymes in familiar books

- Plays simple make-believe games
- Builds towers of four or more blocks
- Might use one hand more than the other
- Follows two-step directions like, "Pick up your shoes and put them in the closet"

36 months
- Can work toys with buttons, levers, and moving parts
- Plays make-believe with dolls, animals, and people
- Does puzzles with three or four pieces
- Understands what "two" means
- Copies a circle with a pencil or crayon
- Turns book pages one at a time
- Builds towers of more than six blocks
- Screws and unscrews jar lids or turns door handles

"You and Erika should review it at home because I have a final recommendation. Cassandra is too young to know the difference between males and females, but she calls you Daddy and Erika Momma. Be aware that she'll start asking questions once she plays with other children, and she'll be ready for that as soon as she begins to walk.

"I recommend you join a Mother and Daughter Support Group. Get a recommendation from the adoption agency. Now, do you have any final questions or comments?"

Erika stood, which signaled Terri to do the same and then said, "I shouldn't have cut you off. Please accept my apology.

Dr. Gerber stood to shake Terri's hand first before ending the session.

"Cassandra is fortunate to have such caring parents, just as you are fortunate to have such a special daughter. Unless an emergency arises, I should examine her in about a year to measure if what continues to emerge is as special as we think. Now go home and have fun playing with her.

Terri spoke for herself as well as for Erika.

"Thanks for everything, doctor. We're about to take your advice."

Chapter 8
April 2234

"Mixing It Up"

Terri kept her promise not to pester Erika about project topics during the break, but she could tell from Erika's frustrated look unless playing with Cassie that she was making little progress.

Erika said nothing to Terri, but she contacted the only person she wanted to the night before Terri would return to the office.

Electra's avatar appeared, waiting for Erika to speak.

"I have news you'll want to tell Indira. Cassie's evaluation at the pediatrician's office confirms what we expected. My daughter is healthy, happy, and gifted physically and mentally.

"Excellent. Indira and I expected much the same. So, why do you look so glum?"

"I visited Monet and Alonzo for additional insights into the Ambassadors Project, which they gave, but even after surfing the web for more info, I've made zero progress turning them into something tangible for Terri. What should I do?"

"Let me do it for you."

The sound of the printer startled her, and when it finally stopped, she retrieved a stack of papers. Electra spoke before she could begin scanning them.

"I have prepared Terri's Project Action Plan. Don't be intimidated by the lengthy background information section. It contains more than enough information for Monet to lead the actual work. You and Terri need concern yourselves only with the

action plan and the who does what sections.

Electra waited for Erika to skim through them, ready to answer the question she knew Erika would pose.

Project Action Plan for Assignment:
The Superpowers Battle for Indigenous People

Background Information
Superpowers: The Nations that Control World Order
Needed for These Reasons:
The world needs superpower nations for several key reasons:
1. **Global stability and security**

2. **Economic leadership:**

3. **Problem-solving capacity.**

4. **Shaping international norms and institutions**

5. **Promoting ideological visions.**

6. **Technological advancement**

7. **Cultural influence**

Superpowers Must Avoid Four Traps:
1. **Thucycides Trap: Every Rising Super Power will challenge the Leader.**

2. **Tacitus Trap: The People of a Rising Super Power will not trust the Government.**

3. **Middle Income Trap: A Rising Super Power, when reaching a certain Income Level, gets stuck there.**

4. **Kindleberger Trap: A Rising Super Power won't invest enough in supporting an International World Order.**

America's Challenge:
- **Diplomatically navigating a multipolar world**

- **Balancing diverse Interests**

- **Maintaining superiority**

TIMELESS TRUTHS FOR THE UNITED STATES GOVERNMENT

Government leaders must pay attention to the following if America is to survive long-term:

Per Samuel Huntington's "Clash of Civilizations":
- Future wars will be fought not between countries, but between these dominant cultures: Western, Confucian, Japanese, Islamic, Hindu, Slavic Orthodox, Latin American, and African

Per Edward Gibbons' "Decline and Fall of the Roman Empire":
- Decline comes gradually until the public wakes up.
- Internal Factors more important than External.
- Beware of Political Corruption and Cultural Decadence.

Per de Tocqueville, Huntington, Rawls, and Rorty:
- Americans are Pragmatic, want Minimal Government, and value Equal Treatment and Diversity
- Modernity's rational "Enlightenment" conflicts with "Classical Humanity"

Key Takeaways for Prolonging America's Reign:
- Maintaining Democracy Requires Constant Vigilance.
- Keep DC Pragmatic and Multi-Partisan
- Let Defeated Enemies maintain control their Countries but put Trusted People in Place and maintain a Military Presence.
- Promise to Protect Allies from External and Internal Threats.
- Extend Citizenship to all Immigrants.
- Leave People with enough Money after taxation to make even more next year.
- Balance "Ruthless Capitalism" against "Empathy-Building Humanism"

Indian-African Econo-Political Alliance
Purpose: To become the next Super Power.
Rationale:

1. African countries and India have similar holistic, ethnic cultures.

2. Both have youthful, growing populations. (Demographics is Destiny).

3. Both have growing middle classes that are ideal consumer-oriented trading partner markets.

4. Their democratic-leaning governments, though not as efficient as the West; they are similar and can shore up each other.

5. Other Third-World / Developing Nations might prefer the Alliance instead of America's or China's Super Power Poles.

6. A Multi-Polar International Structure should be more Inclusive and Equitable than the Current Bi-Polar One.

7. Indian and African Nations' relative strengths compensate for each other's relative weaknesses.

India's Rel. Strengths	Africa's Rel. Strengths
Tech. Transfer	Raw Mat. (Oil Rare Earth)
Dir. Inv. Capital	Cropland/Food
Flood Control Eng.	

Alliance can bargain better than separately with the two Super Powers.

The Changing World Order Says
Washington's Political Game is Almost Over!

- **Symptoms: Look at Current Events!**

- **World Order Changes According to Predictable 200-250 Year Cycles (Rise Peak Decline) that overlap for 20-40 Years. Current Cycle labeled "American World Order." Overlap is rife with Conflict/Uncertainty. It marks transition from Current Leading Nation to Next.**

- **Internal Conflicts caused by Inequality. External Conflicts caused by Rising Nation confronting Current Leader.**

Wars start Cycles. Victory goes to Nation with More Power than Rival. Victor dictates Rules of New World Order.

- **Leader of Victor initially obtains Power via Revolution and then: Consolidates it by eliminating those who oppose; Establishes System and Institutions to make Strong Internal**

Government; Builds Military; Grows Capital Market by uniting Government, Military, and Important Companies; Determines best way to pick Successor of Leader.

1. Eight Factors control Cycle by determining Power of Leading Nation: 1.Education and Work Ethic of People

2. People's Inventiveness/Technology

3. Economic Competitiveness

4. Economic Output

5. Share of Trade

6. Military Strength

7. Strength of Financial Center

8. Strength of Currency so it's World Reserve

Note that Factor 1 comprises: Leadership Character   Rule of Law   Low Corruption
Resource Efficiency   Openness to Glob. Ideas
Factor1 is the causal factor for Factor 2, etc.
These markers run sequentially along the arc from
left to right:

1. **New World Order Cycle begins. This begins the Cycle's Rise.**

2. **Peace, Prosperity, and Productivity reign at Home and spill into World.**

3. **Leading Nation uses Debt to fuel Productive Growth.**

   This marks the Peak, but the Peak sows the seeds for the

   decline: People become too expensive and lose their jobs

> to Foreigners; People get "lazy" and lose their competitive edge; People want to consume more and work less; Children of Wealthy People aren't "tough."

4. Debt leads to Financial Bubble that causes Big Wealth Gap and then Bursts.

5. Other Nations copy what works and they become wealthy and competitive.

6. Leading Nation over-reaches and causes Financial Bubble that bursts, leading to Economic collapse. This begins the Decline.

7. Leading Nation prints Money and lives off Credit from Other Nations. A Rising Nation emerges; it will become the Next Leading Nation.

8. Hardships lead to Leading Nation's Internal Revolution.

   External Challenge caused by Rising Nation seizing opportunity to dethrone Leading Nation.

9. Confrontation leads to War. Current Leading Nation Defeated and Next Leading Nation along with its Allies force debt and political restructuring on loser.

10. Another New World Order Cycle begins.

What are the reasons for the decline of the American World Order?
CONGRESS IS TO BLAME! HERE'S WHY:

- Collapse of Congress's civility and its inability to compromise lead to Legislative gridlock and derangement.

- Congress transitions from a Legislative Institution into a Delegator of Legislative Power that it gives to unelected bureaucratic State Agencies containing Subject Matter Experts. This Transition is the biggest threat to Democracy!

- America's Founding Fathers wanted to avoid legislative tyranny by having a Representative Government whose form would link Politician's self-interest to People's Public

Interest / Common Good. They thought they could rein in Human Nature by setting up a Congressional legislative body that would uphold the Constitution by balancing the Executive, Legislative, and Judicial branches.

- But Congress can't handle the complications and complexities of the Issues it must legislate. It needs Subject Matter Experts who can analyze problems and recommend decisions.

- So, Congress dumps Legislative Power into Regulatory Agencies! (Founding Father Thomas Jefferson expected Congress would suck in Power from Executive and Judicial branches, but instead it delegates Power to unelected bureaucratic SMEs. Jefferson misread human nature!

Legislators will never ditch the Seven Deadly sins! They are merely human!

- CONSTITUTION IS OK, BUT AMERICA NEEDS A NEW FORM OF GOVERNMENT TO IMPLEMENT IT! THINK OF CONSTITUTION AS A MISSION STATEMENT, AND THE FORM OF GOVERNMENT AS THE INSTRUMENT FOR CARRYING OUT A PLAN TO MAKE THE CONSTITUTION REFLECT THE WILL OF THE PEOPLE.

Pequot Indian Nation's Role:
The Pequot Indian Nation is ideally suited to lead the formation of the National American Indian Alliance (NAIA) because of its economic and technological strengths. It will recruit Native American Tribal Nations that meet its standards.
Recommended Constitution:
Include these components in a simplified U.S. Constitution:
- Primacy of the Individual rather than the State.

- Respect for all Races, Sexes. Religions, Ethnicities, and Genders.

- **Endorses Holistic Philosophical Approach where practical.**
- **Freedom to choose Lifestyle.**
- **Equal Opportunity to compete for Education and Career.**
- **Inalienable Rights to Healthcare and Viable Income.**
- **Progress driven by Technological Innovation mining Big Data.**

Recommended Government:
Republican form of Government consisting of:

1. Unicameral legislature (one house called the House of Delegates) containing one member from each agreed-upon District. Delegates decided from at most three candidates by ranked-choice voting of People. Winners are those with the highest tallies. Delegates can serve only one six-year term.

2. An elected President and an elected Vice President decided from at least three and no more than five political parties by ranked-choice voting of the People. Winners are those with the highest tallies. President or Vice President can serve at most two four-year terms.

3. A group of nine selected from a pool of twenty Subject Matter Experts designated by the President. The nine will be picked by ranked-choice voting of the Delegates. Voting occurs every six years. The SMEs can serve a maximum of eight years.

4. Democratic or Socialistic forms emphasizing Equality Under the Law for all Social Classes; Authoritarian, Tyrannical, or Oligarchic forms excluded.

- **Endorses a Capitalistic, Free-Market, and Price-Driven Economy supported by Meritocracy rather than "Favoritism".**
- **Puts in place Public Ownership, Taxation, and Service Systems for promoting the Greater Good while avoiding the Tragedy of the Commons.**
- **Provides Social Safety Nets to minimize Economic Inequality.**

- Acknowledges that all forms of Discrimination are driven by Social, not Genetic characteristics, and works to minimize or eliminate via Diversity, Equity, and Inclusion initiatives.
- Uses Technological Progress for Environment and Population Protection.
- Seeks Pragmatic Compromise rather than Ideological Solutions.
- Willing to recognize other Nations that pose no threat.

Native American Indian Alliance (NAIA) Criteria:
1. Member Nations must be Native American Indian Democratic, Republic, Libertarian, or Socialistic Governments and not Authoritarian, Tyrannical, or Oligarchical.

2. Each Member Nation self-governs.

3. The first Leading Nation of the NAIA is the Pequot Nation. As Member Nations are added, a Security Council of at most seven members will elect by ranked-choice voting every four years the Leading Nation.

4. The NAIA will provide protection against external threats to any Member Nation.

Nations/Organizations Impacted
- India, Zimbabwe, NAIA, IPWA

Action Plan:
- Travel to Washington, DC to interview Connecticut Senators and Representatives, NAIA and IPWA Headquarters, African and Indian Embassies.

- Create thirty-minute video using interviews and stock footage.

Who Does What:
- Erika and Team Researcher add to Background Information.

- Alonzo coordinates Travel and Logistics.

- **Film Crew selects Stock Footage.**
- **Terri writes Voice-over Script and Film Crew edits Interviews into the Video.**
- **Mario approves the final cut and reviews it with Mrs. Harmony by the first week of April.**

Erika did so a minute later, after flipping through the background information.

"What do I tell Terri?"

"That she has plenty of information to impress Mario and Mrs. Harmony, and the team researcher needs no help from you, which frees up your and Terri's time."

Erika's delight showed in her smile.

"Hooray, everyone wins. And I promise to dig into the information enough to help Monet when we get to that stage."

"Excellent plan. Now think about what you'll say to Terri when she comes home from work tomorrow."

Electra's avatar disappeared before Erika could thank her, but she did follow her advice.

When Terri came home from work the next day, Erika had everything ready before Terri joined them in the kitchen. Erika spoke first.

"No need to ask how our day went. It was even better than yesterday, and here's why."

She handed her three hefty copies of the Project Plan while talking.

"Don't worry about all the background info. That's essentially for Monet, and it'll impress the bosses. All you have to worry about are the last two sections, which should be no worry at all."

Erika busied herself with Cassie while Terri skimmed the document.

By the time she finished, her expression showed pure joy.

"This is amazing. How'd you do it?"

"That's my job, and we're set until Alonzo puts us and the team on the road. Mario can stay in the office."

"Thanks to you, I can cruise at the office, and you can do likewise at home. Now let's eat."

Cruising meant Erika tried to take Cassie to the next level by helping her overcome gravity via walking, which her first steps a week later did.

Meanwhile, Terri took midday workouts at the fitness center and thought about what she could buy for Erika and Cassie.

Erika's cell phone chime interrupted Cassie's walking session several days later. The building's front desk security guard notified that a delivery person had something for Terri Tarrant. Erika gave permission for the driver to deliver it, and greeted him in the hallway.

"Do you know what it is?"

"It's an electronic sound mixer like recording studios use. Where do you want me to put it?"

"Right where you are. I'll unpack and bring it in.

"Be sure to read the instruction manual before plugging all the parts together. Most people plug first and read later.

"Good advice. Thanks."

Erika took the parts into the family room, where she could talk to Cassie while reading and assembling.

"Look what we have: a control box, a keyboard, and a monitor. The keyboard and monitor plug into the control box, which has lots of levers and buttons for mixing inputs. I'll plug them together, but I won't turn it on until we read the instructions and look at on-line videos."

Terri followed the sound of music into the family room when she came home, finding Erika tapping Cassie's fingers on the keyboard. Mother and daughter stopped playing and gazed at her.

"Sounds like you know what you're doing. How do you like my educational present?"

"It's wonderful. I learned enough to run the mixer, and Cassie loves making music when she taps the keys, but why'd you buy it?"

"Don't you know that listening to or playing music makes us smarter? And learning to play a musical instrument is great training for kids. You can play and teach piano to Cassie and yourself at the same time.

Erika added,

"And when she's old enough, we can hire a music teacher. Hey, I've got an idea. Why don't we take an online music appreciation class? That way, we'll know more about classical as well as rock music, and I can tell Cassie about the music in the background whenever we're playing."

"That's good. It'll also help me assemble a mix of pop songs I can listen to while working out.

"Nice idea. Why don't you take Cassie and me to meet your fitness trainer sometime? You can show him your mix, and he can show us the daycare room.

"OK, we'll do it before Alonzo takes us away."

Chapter 9
April 2234

"A Jolting Hit on the DC Trip"

Terri took Erika and Cassie to the health club a week before Alonzo would drive the team to conduct interviews in Washington.

She made the introductions while Erika and Cassie stood next to her.

"Erika, this is Jocko Eze, my fitness coach. And Jocko, this is my roommate Erika Kincaid and her daughter Cassie. They want to see the daycare room after watching you take me through my training routine."

"That'll be jim-dandy whether I spell it J I M or G Y M, so let's get started."

Erika watched but spoke only to herself while keeping Cassie in front of her.

Wow, what a good-looking guy; his attempt at humor seemed genuine, and he's definitely interested in Terri.

When Terri's training session ended forty-five minutes later, Jocko gave them a daycare room tour, and when finished said,

"How about me and my roommate Jimmy take you out to dinner the day after tomorrow at a place near the health club? We can meet here at six and walk to the place."

"I like that. Can Erika bring Cassie?"

"Why not? She can eat some ice cream or whatever else Erika picks. See ya then."

Terri and her entourage went to the women's locker room and then walked home. While walking, Terri joked,

"You're getting your exercise by pushing that industrial-strength baby stroller you bought a while ago. It's large enough to carry a suitcase along with Cassie."

"Maybe so, but I think you better get more exercise by pushing Jocko farther away.

Terry yanked Erika to a stop.

"What's that supposed to mean?"

"I think he's ready to hit on you, and you're the one who warned me about the risks long ago.

"Well, maybe I want him to. I haven't had a serious date since I don't know when. You haven't either. Don't you miss it?"

"You like sex more than I do. I'm happy with things the way they are.

"Well if I date him, it won't change things for us, at least not right away.

"Perhaps not, so do what you want."

The duo followed their normal routines all the way to dinner with the guys. Terri sat next to Jocko and Erika on the other side of the booth, holding Cassie on her lap next to Jimmy. The conversation flowed smoothly until Jocko caressed Terri's hands while saying,

"I think you're a special lady. You've got a strong mind and body. Why don't we get to know each other better?"

"Gosh, I don't know." Terri's few words left an embarrassing pause in the conversation that Erika filled.

"She's had experiences in the past with fellows who were bad, so take it easy.

Jimmy tried to hype his presence by saying,

"Whatcha mean by that? Has she been—"

Erika yelled to stop his words from touching on something better left unsaid.

"Are you a complete idiot? Don't go where you don't belong. Dinner's over for me and Cassie.

As Erika stood to leave, Jocko tried to salvage the evening by saying,

"Please wait. Don't judge me by the other guys. They're not me. Just give me a chance.

Terri rose, then said,

"Let me think about it," before the duo walked away.

The night air cooled Erika enough to listen to Terri.

"You sure put those guys in their places. Maybe you're right. I'll shelve the idea until we come back from DC.

"Good, and I apologize if you think I spoke out of turn, but I have only your best interests at heart.

"I know that." Terri's kiss on Erika's cheek needed no additional words.

All the details fell into place for Sunday's five-hour drive from New York City to Wahington, DC. Terri sat next to Alonzo as he cruised on Interstate 95 and let him explain the schedule to the crew who occupied the two bench seats behind.

"We've got four interviews with senators and congresspeople from the states Terri picked and four on Tuesday with the NAIA and IPWA organizations, plus two with African embassies. Monet knows about this. She'll be part of the follow-up if the interviews go well, so why don't you include her on Tuesday?"

"I didn't think of that, but that should be easy.

"And we'll drive back Tuesday evening, which should also be easy. It'll be after the DC traffic clears. Does anyone have anything else to say?"

No one did, so the crew rehearsed for the rest of the trip while Erika gazed at the scenery streaming by.

Monday unfolded according to plan. Erika stood out of the way and observed how all the congresspeople seemed to preen with both words and body language for the camera.

Nothing unexpected happened on Tuesday, so Alonzo went through a McDonald's drive-thru to save time. Terri placed the order from the front row's passenger seat and paid for the entire crew.

Light traffic and cloud-streaked skies on a moonlit night added to the festive atmosphere in the van. The crew chief's comparison between recent assignments entertained the riders.

"I doubt a tsunami or some such catastrophe will hit us on the drive back, but just to be safe, I've already uploaded all the videos, so is something happens, they're already home.

The crew exchanged small talk until everyone had said enough before withdrawing into their personal spaces. Alonzo paid enough attention to the road ahead while letting thoughts of Monet fill the rest, but a jolt brought him back when a van rammed from behind. Trying to break away, he slammed the pedal to the floor while yelling,

"Everyone, buckle up. We're gonna—," but another jolt stopped his words, and he couldn't break away this time.

Having more horsepower, the ramming van smashed into the van's left rear corner panel, lifting its rear wheels off the pavement.

Alonzo jerked the steering wheel to the right just as I-95 curved to the left, but it force multiplied the spin even more, hooking bumpers, tipping both vans onto their sides, and rolling them down an embankment.

The ramming van exploded before coming to a dead stop. Alonzo's came to rest on its side, driver's side up, just far enough away to avoid being incinerated by the flames mushrooming every which way.

He yelled,

"Climb out if you can; help anyone who can't.

He followed his advice by pulling out an unconscious Terri. She had blood streaming from a gash on the side of her face, caused by bouncing her head into the windshield.

Clutching her laptop, Erika crawled through the sliding door opening and stood aside as all remaining passengers clambered out. The smell of gasoline energized everyone to huddle around Alonzo as he and Erika propped up a semi-conscious Terri. He shouted,

"Follow me and run like hell."

They reached the pavement just before their van burst into flames. All but Alonzo and Erika stood like zombies, staring at the surreal sight.

Alonzo ripped off his shirt and started wiping Terri's cheek.

"She won't bleed to death, but the cut'll need stitches.

Flashing headlights and a blaring horn turned his attention to the van that came screeching to a halt only yards away. When recognizing the driver who had leaped out, Alonzo yelled,

"Jump into the backup van. We gotta get away before the state troopers get here.

Alonzo sat next to Elton Bose and kept dabbing Terri's gash. Erika used her laptop to locate the nearest emergency room. By the time Alonzo and Erika took Terri inside, the rest of the team had returned to life and stayed in the van.

Erika and Alonzo sat in the waiting room, sipping cans of Coke Alonzo bought from the vending machine. The chase and rescue had drained their adrenaline, so they sat silently. Alonzo dozed fitfully, but Erika talked to herself.

Lord love Alonzo and Elton. Everyone's safe. Only Terri came away injured, but she'll heal. Who tried to kill us, and why? There's only one person to ask, and I'll do that as soon as we're home.

Chapter 10
April 2234

"Secret Weapons at the Ready"

Terri gave the entire team the day off but forced herself to meet with Mario and Mrs. Harmony, so she could explain the attack that hit on the drive back. After Mario set up the online meeting, she gave a reporter-like summary. Mrs. Harmony gave her comments first.

"Have the film crew edit in the attack. Be sure to include close-ups showing your stitches. That'll build even more viewer empathy.

"But what about the attack? What about future risks and dangers?"

Mario gave his answer.

"Everyone faces risks just by living. Attacks on reporters have happened before and no doubt they'll happen again. Your guy Alonzo did good; hire him on all future projects.

Mario's pause let Mrs. Harmony segue in.

"And here's your next assignment. I watched a chilling PBS documentary called "The Poles Revealed". Watch it and then develop a project that connects to the one you just did. We'll give you to Memorial Day for the final cut. That should be plenty of time. You and that ghostwriter partner of yours are clever and resilient, and the video crew likes your style.

Removing most of Terri's fatigue, Mrs. Harmony's compliment showed in Terri's confident voice.

"I'll tell Erika, and we'll make it happen."

While Terri's meeting was taking place, so was Erika's.

After logging on to her home workstation with Cassie at her side, she invoked Electra's avatar and gave a blow-by-blow description of the entire DC trip. When finished, she asked what Electra knew was coming.

"Who do you think attacked us?"

"Think back to the attack that blew up Mrs. Walthers' car. You suspected a mole at the New York Times. Perhaps there's one at IBN, or perhaps, as Alonzo said, some government agencies or their corporate cronies don't like Terri stepping on their toes. And your genetic predecessors considered conspiracy theories to explain attacks. Perhaps there are –"

Erika's rising agitation showed as she interrupted.

"But is there something you can do to help?"

The answer came with the whirring of Erika's printer. She retrieved two pages and read for enough minutes until Electra spoke.

Agent-Based Socio-Political Forecasting Model

It is Objective Statistical Forecasting software that utilizes Big Data via synthesis of Regression and Correlation.

It analyzes data from these categories for Specified Countries, Organizations or Persons of Interest:
- Military Ranking
- GDP Ranking
- Population Ranking
- Government Factor: 1(Authoritarian) to 10 (Democratic)
- DEI Factor: 1(Repressive) to 10 (Permissive)
- Belligerence Factor: 1(War-Mongering) 10(Peace-Loving)
- Political Goal:
1. Achieve Superpower Status
2. Maintain Current Position
3. Seek Alliances
- Social Goal:

1. More Repressive
2. Maintain Current Position
3. More Permissive

The software is my proprietary software that exceeds the best forecasting models coming from "Mere Mortals".

It outputs a forecast for these categories:
- **Future Relationship between Specified Countries**
- **Political Goal**
- **Social Goal**
- **Probability of Success**

The output forecasts each category.

To run this software, use this Graphical User Interface:

Agent-Based Socio-Political Forecasting

First Country: _______________   Second Country: __________
Organization   Organization
Or Person   Or Person
Time Horizon: One Year__ Five Years__Ten Years___ _____

Press the Enter Key or the Screen after entering your choices above. The Forecast will appear on the screen in this format:

Future Relationship: Written or Audio

Political Goal: Written or Audio

Social Goal: Written or Audio

Probability of Success: Written or Audio

"I don't expect you to know enough to understand the underlying details, but you don't need to. If the need arises, I shall run it and then give you a useful summary of the output.

"You're sure this can help?"

"What did I just say?"

"I'm sorry. I know better, but sometimes I forget. Please accept my apology.

Electra's consoling tone made her words even gentler.

"No need to. I see a marked improvement in many aspects of your personality.

Having been suitably chastised and then forgiven, Erika asked,

"Do you think I'll ever know enough to run the app myself?"

"Perhaps in the future, but don't concern yourself about it. Now get back to your present.

Electra vanished. Erika took Cassie to the kitchen for a snack.

When Terri stepped into the kitchen after coming home, Erika thought she wore a happily tired look, prompting her to ask,

"Did your bosses say something nice about the videos?"

"They complimented us for how we handled the attack, and they want us to put it in the video. Me and the crew can handle that, but I need your help on the next assignment. They want us to come up with a topic that connects the Arctic regions to our last podcast.

"Huh?"

"They say we're clever, and Mrs. Harmony told us to watch a PBS documentary called "The Poles Revealed. Why don't we do it after supper? Then maybe it'll make more sense, and Cassie will learn something. I'm sure you can find it on the web.

"OK, that'll make for a relaxing evening.

The trio started watching two one-hour episodes until Cassie fell asleep. Erika returned after putting her to bed, and they watched the second one to the end.

Terri spoke as soon as it finished.

"People should watch those documentaries only when the Sun and temperature are in the people-friendly zone. The poles are amazingly hostile environments for most species. I feel like cocooning in a thermal blanket and sleeping until the Sun wakes me. What's your take?"

"It takes a special person to work in Antarctica. The video touched on psychiatric counseling, but I think people working there suffer from depression or worse. I'd go crazy being cooped up twenty-four-seven for countless days when a storm hits.

"Did you notice how few women work there? What d'you think that says about women's equality?"

"I think few females would want to work there. Modern technology has greatly reduced the physical requirements for most jobs, and women are just as qualified except for those requiring brute strength.

"I think you're right. Females are often better equipped cognitively and emotionally than men, but what's your take on the physical dimension?"

"Elemental survival of the fittest. Look at it this way. If your team had to pull a loaded sled through a howling blizzard, do you think many females could pull their weight? Neither of us could. And the photos of the early explorers showed how tough they had it. No wonder they looked broken down and weather-beaten with the skin of a hundred-year-old. Please don't plan any Antarctic assignments.

"I won't, but does the documentary give you any ideas about what Mrs. Harmony wants?"

Erika shook her head before saying,

"Nope. I better think about it. And speaking of thinking, have you thought more about dating Jocko?"

"Not until I get the stitches out and cover the scar with cosmetics.

Terri moved face-to-face before asking,

"How does the scar look? You think it might fade away?"

"It might, but if it doesn't, it'll add intrigue to your persona, and in some Middle Eastern cultures, they're considered beauty marks."

"OK, if you say so, but let's get back to our next assignment. Mario's giving us until the end of May to finish the video, but he needs to see our Project Action Plan ASAP. Please do me a favor and assemble something I can show within the next few days."

"OK, I'll start first thing tomorrow."

The next morning, Erika kept Cassie on her lap or at her side while looking for information that might trigger an idea for the plan, but she found nothing helpful. After lunch, she contacted Electra, talking first.

"Terri's bosses liked how her crew handled everything on the last assignment, including our escape from attackers. But they gave her a vague assignment to connect the last one – which is called 'The Superpowers Battle for Indigenous People' – to the Arctic regions. They gave the end of May as a final cut deadline and told her to watch a PBS documentary called 'The Poles Revealed' for ideas on something specific. Her boss wants the Project Action Plan ASAP. I spent all morning searching for more info but struck out. Would it be possible for you to give me some suggestions? I'm asking only because the deadline's too tight, but I promise to strengthen my skills so I don't have to ask in the future unless it's a dire emergency.

Electra said,

"I will do better than that." Milliseconds later, the printer whirred.

Project Action Plan for Assignment:
The Superpowers Battle for The
Poles Background Information

Arctic Regions
- **Antarctica and the Oceans are Earth's Last Frontiers.**
- **They contain Earth's Geographic Poles.**
- **In 1907, U.S. Admiral Peary won Race to North Pole.**
- **In 1911, Britain's Robert Scott and Norway's Roald Amundsen launched expeditions to reach the South Pole. Amundsen won but Scott's Expedition perished.**
- **Science Background**
- **Earth composed of Layers: Inner Core Outer Core Mantle Crust.**
- **Continents float on Tectonic Plates, which float on Outer Core.**

- Earth's Inner Core is Solid Metal; Outer Core is Liquid Metal; Earth's Rotation about its Axis makes Earth a Gigantic Bar Magnet with Magnetic Field diving into the Earth at North and South Poles.

- Antarctic ice rests upon an actual Continent. Arctic ice has no underlying Continent. This imbalance causes the Earth's rotational axis to precess (rotate) with a period of 25.7 thousand years. Rotational axis tilted 23.4° angular offset (obliquity) between the Earth's axis of rotation and a perpendicular to the Earth's orbital plane with the Sun.

- Rotational Tilt causes Change of Seasons. Precession causes Magnetic Field location to change. Magnetic Fields and ocean currents cause periodic Global Warming and Cooling (Ice Ages)

- Oceans store heat oxygen, and carbon dioxide..

- Interactions among Sun, Atmosphere, Oceans, and Magnetic Field cause Climate Change.

- Current Conjecture: Man's Pollution into the Environment (Heat from burning Fossil Fuels and plastics/toxic chemicals dumped into Oceans) cause Climate Change and threaten other species.

Socio-Political-Economic Background
- Major Nations want to mine resources from the Antarctic.

- Major Nations want to study how species and equipment can survive in Antarctic's extreme climate (like living on Mars or in Outer Space or on the Ocean Floor).

- Seven countries (Argentina, Australia, Chile, France, New Zealand, Norway, and the United Kingdom)

- WHOEVER MASTERS THE ANTARCTIC WILL CONTROL THE FUTURE!

Action Plan:
- No travel required. Conduct Online Interviews with Key U.S. Geophysical Agency Scientists and NASA/DOD Departments, Ambassadors from Countries Battling for Antarctic Supremacy (U.S. Russia China India)

- **Create thirty-minute video using interviews and stock footage**

Who Does What:
- **Erika and Team Researcher add to Background Information.**

- **Film Crew selects Stock Footage.**

- **Terri writes Voice-Over Script and Film Crew edits Interviews into the Video.**

- **Mario approves the final cut and reviews it with Mrs. Harmony by the end of May.**

Electra waited for Erika to respond, which she did after skimming what had been printed.

"I know better than to ask how you do this, so all I'll say is thank you for freeing my time and giving Terri something her bosses will love.

"You are welcome; here are three more copies for Terri. Now carry on.

Soon after Electra's avatar vanished, Erika heard a tiny voice say, "Momma, who you talk to?"

She picked up Cassie to rub noses before answering.

"Why that's Electra, my Cyber Mentor-Mother. She's a very-very special person we talk to only on the computer. She's like a secret helper and weapon. And only we know about her. You must promise me you'll never tell our secret to anyone.

"I promise.

"Why thank you. Now, let's go play some music."

The Project Action Plan worked even better than Terri's wildest hopes. Mario loved it, giving her carte blanche authority when implementing the plan, and both Terri and Erika had more time for other activities.

Erika talked via an online conference call with Monet and Alonzo to summarize Terri's project and to ask Monet when she would need her help on the Ambassadors project.

"Sometime in June. I'm still negotiating with my contacts.

"I'll be ready.

Alonzo ended the call with his cheery words.

"And I'm ready whenever you and Terri need my logistics and security services. Just let me know.

Alonzo's last words regarding security services sparked one of Erika's dormant thoughts.

If trouble comes my way, I need something stronger than harsh words or pepper spray. Terri lost the gun we used to carry several adventures ago. It's about time I replace it in a manner that no one will know, and I know how to do that. I'm going to the Deep-Dark Web.

Once there, she searched for a gun that would meet her requirements: light, compact, accurate, magazine-and-silencer equipped, and untraceable. An hour later, she purchased a 3-D-printed Glock revolver, two magazines, a silencer, and an ample supply of bullets. Then she made plans to pick them up.

I don't want the Government or any of the "Bad Guys" to know what I'm doing. That's why my computer has encryption software, I have a private Bitcoin wallet, and I'm browsing with TOR, the onion-routing browser. TOR handles anonymous web surfing and protection against traffic analysis.

And I never give my name, address, or phone number to anyone, which means I have to pick up the stuff anonymously by going to an un-disclosed distribution center and using the purchase code to verify I'm the actual buyer.

I now know the center's location, the date my stuff will be there, and my purchase code. So, the only thing left is to go there alone when no one knows what I'm up to, not even Terri.

I'll slip away sometime next week when she's looking after Cassie and no one will miss me. And when I come back, I put the stuff in a private place that only I know. All this is training me to be a better spy than ever before, and I'll soon be even better at handling whatever's in store.

Chapter 11
June 2234

"Toxic Clouds in the Way"

Even though Terri said she didn't need help at the final cut meeting, Erika invited herself in case the bosses asked questions Terri couldn't handle, and she also wanted to hear what they said, not afterward when filtered through Terri.

Mrs. Harmony let Mario start the meeting.

"Our market research indicates viewers loved how you connected the latest video – 'Superpowers Battling for the Poles' –

to the previous one, which was Superpowers Battling for Indigenous People. They liked your presentation style and command of the background information. They particularly liked the link between Climate Change and Earth's magnetic field. Could you tell us a bit more about it?"

Terri's inchoate look of confusion triggered Erika to answer.

"Terri knows a lot about it, but she has too much going on to remember all the details. That's my job, so let me give you more.

Erika's min-lecture lasted just long enough for Mrs. Harmony, who directed her comments toward Terri.

"I've heard plenty. You two make IBN's best team. No wonder the viewers love you. Try fitting Erika into your next video. You can pick the topic, but make sure it has that up-close-and in-person touch showing danger and risk.

Terri's "in-command" expression returned.

"We'll to it. What's our completion date for the final cut?"

"No later than the end of July."

"We'll make it so by starting now."

Terri stayed at the office to network with the crew while Erika went to pick up Cassie.

That night after dinner, Terri and Erika discussed potential topics while Cassie played with the mixer's keyboard.

Terri's apologetic look accompanying her words started the conversation.

"Thanks for bailing me out. I don't know what I was going to say about magnetic fields. From now on, please come to all the boss's meetings. You can even bring Cassie.

"That's a deal. And how about this? I'll research topics for what Mrs. Harmony wants and draft an action plan you can show Mario by Friday."

"If you do that, I'll play with Cassie whenever you need a break and I'm home.

"That'll work for the three of us. How about I start tonight?"

"If it's good by you, it's good by me."

Erika decided not to seek help from Electra but instead allowed her growing self-confidence to take command. She printed four copies of Terri's next Action Plan and then took them to Terri on Thursday evening.

Project Action Plan for Assignment: The World Health Crisis

Background Information
People's Health Status
- Potential Viral Pandemics caused by New or Mutant Viruses

- Poor Nutrition: Too much Meat and Junk Food Consumption, Too little Fruit and Vegetable Consumption in the U.S.

- Lack of Exercise

- Prevalent Diseases: Obesity, Diabetes, High Bood Pressure, Heart Attacks, Cancer

- Old Age Diseases: Arthritis, Dementia/Alzheimer's

Worldwide Food Supply Status
- Disappearance of Farmlands

- Bird and Animal Populations Susceptible to Zoonotic Viral Outbreaks transmitted to Humans

- Shortage of Animal Protein

Action Plan:
- Limited Travel Required: Interview via online audio-visual software: Key U.S. Geophysical Agency Scientists and NASA/DOD Departments, and Ambassadors from Nations suffering from Food Insecurity (India and African Nations)

- Create a thirty-minute video using interviews and stock footage

Who Does What:
- Terri and the Team Researcher add to Background Information and identify which Ambassadors and Cultured Meat Processor to include.

- Film Crew selects Stock Footage.

- Terri writes Voice-Over Script and Film Crew edits Interviews into the Video.

- **Terri hires Alonzo for logistics and security and Monet for including with the Ambassadors.**
- **Mario approves final cut and reviews it with Mrs. Harmony by the end of July.**

When she stepped into the family room and started talking after handing her three copies, Terri stopped playing music with Cassie and looked at Erika.

"Here's the next Project Action Plan – 'The World Health Crisis'. All you do is tell the team researcher to flesh out some details for the Background Information section.

After studying the Plan for a couple of minutes, Terri asked the only two questions Erika thought Terri would ask.

"What's a cultured meat processor, and why do an interview there?"

"Cultured meat solves the animal protein shortage. A processing plant synthesizes protein from animal stem cells grown in pressurized industrial-sized vats containing potent bacteria and viruses. Incubators pump in stem cells, bacteria and viruses transform the cells into liquid protein, pumps extract the liquid protein, and feed it into 3-D printers from which bacon strips, hamburger patties, chicken breasts, and steaks emerge. Got it?"

"People can buy them at food stores today, right?"

"Yes, and here's the risk plus danger angle. No matter what they're producing, all processing plants as large as those for commercial cultured meat must have ongoing maintenance to prevent accidents. I'll write that part of your script and handle that interview, OK?"

"You bet. The Plan needs no editing. I'll show it to Mario and the crew tomorrow before contacting Alonzo and Monet. And for your bonus, I'll cook dinners this weekend, using cultured meat.

"Wonderful. I'm ready for a bedtime snack before sacking in. Terri ended the discussion.

"I'll take care of tonight's snack." Please follow me to the kitchen. Erika playfully tugged Cassie in that direction.

Having finished her part of the current project until traveling to a processing plant, Erika turned her attention to playing with her daughter until Cassie needed a nap. While resting next to her, Erika considered what she should do next for Cassie's development.

Now that she's getting so big and strong and smart, it's time to join a mother-daughter support group. I'll arrange for Terri and me to take Ava and Ivana out for dinner to get a recommendation. They'll enjoy seeing how much Cassie's already grown. I call them this evening.

Terri's project work progressed smoothly. Her crew and researcher handled the pieces she delegated, while she arranged for Alonzo and Monet to join them. Once that was done, she set the date for interviewing the processing plant manager. Afterward, she called employees at other plants to arrange interviews for opinions about risks and safety.

The first couple of employees felt uncomfortable talking about these topics for fear of being fired, but she found one who would be willing.

"You can interview me as long as you keep me and the company anonymous. Can you do that?"

"Of course. My video crew will mask your voice and blur your face so no one knows who you are. What day, time, and location work for you…?"

Terri kept calling until she found another one willing.

"Sure, you can interview me, and you can even use my name as well as the company's. It's forcing me to take early retirement, and I wanna call out how this industry overworks its people while undercutting routine maintenance. Doing this can cause all sorts of dangers and risks. And I wanna blow the whistle on terrorist attacks. People should know about unreported attempts at blowing up reactors.

"You're right. That's my job, to let the public know the facts. Please pick a day, time, and place, and me and my crew will be there."

With Erika pushing the stroller, she and Terri strolled into the restaurant Ava had selected. When Ivana waved, Terri led her partner to a booth in the plant-filled rustic eating area. Soft elevator music added to the ambiance.

With Cassie between her and Ivana and Terri and Ava on the opposite side, Erika led the conversation. After typical greetings, she steered the conversation toward her daughter.

"Now that Cassie's big and strong, I'd like to join a mother-daughter support group. Which one would you recommend?"

"My favorite one that meets every day in a nearby daycare center. Your first visit is free, and if you join the group, you pay only a tiny amount each time you go.

"What happens at the meetings?"

"The mothers talk while the kids play; then there's a juice-and-cookies break for the little ones and something stronger for the moms. I'll jot down the address and phone number.

The server took orders as Ava did that, then handed her scribbling to Erika as soon as the server left, and she continued.

"So, what's new in Terri's world?"

"I'm busy working but have enough time for health club workouts. I like my instructor and plan to start dating him. He's – "

Ivana's frown accented the words that interrupted.

"Why you do that? Women much better than men.

That stopped the conversation. Erika restarted it by saying,

"I met the guy. Jocko Eze's a smart, handsome Black guy who looks at most in his late twenties. He sure seems nice enough. Terri, tell us what his name means.

"Glad to. Jocko is a Hebrew word that means 'God is gracious', and Eze is a Nigerian surname meaning 'King'.

Terri stopped because she saw Ivana ready to reply.

"Ha, they all seem nice when they want something, but you never know what they thinking."

No one found the right words to keep the conversation going until Ava said,

"I guess it's Terri's problem to figure out. Ah, here comes our server with the drinks. Let's change the subject."

Erika took Cassie to the Monday morning meeting, listening to the mothers while observing how the girls played. When a break came, she retrieved Cassie before cornering the group leader.

"I like your style and want to sign up. How does my almost two-year-old look?"

She's big for her age and gets along with the other girls. Her social skills will develop even faster if you bring her several times each week.

"That's why we're joining, and I think having a pet would help her develop even faster. You think she's too young?"

"Many moms ask that question, and I tell them four years is the lower limit for most kids. But each is different, so I tell them to consider these issues – did the child ask for a pet? If she did, explain what she must do to take care of it, and you better be ready to take over when she can't. And remember, pets affect the entire family, so don't make a snap decision.

"Thanks, that's really helpful. I'm sure both Cassie and I will learn a lot at future meetings. See you then."

Erika and Terry kept pleasantly busy with personal activities for the rest of the week. Erika took Cassie to Ava's place on Saturday so she could take care of her while she and Terri were traveling for interviews.

Terri worked out at the health club, letting Jocko chat her up until the entire crew loaded into Alonzo's van outside the office on Sunday afternoon

Alonzo repeated the agenda while driving.

"On Monday, we interview people at the government agencies and embassies that Terri and Monet picked. Make sure you get both of them in the video. Then we drive early Tuesday to interview the one employee at each plant who agreed to the interview. Clear so far?"

No one nodded yes or no, so he continued.

"Erika does the interviewing. Make sure you set up the cameras close enough to the containment building to show the scale of the place, but far enough away so plant guards don't see us. We do one in the morning and one in the afternoon. Then we drive tomorrow evening and stay in the town close to the plant where its P.R. person gives Erika a tour. Terri and Monica will wait at the motel until we get them for the drive home on Wednesday evening. Any questions?"

None came, so everyone talked about the world health crisis risks, while Erika provided additional information.

Monday's interviews proceeded smoothly, thanks to Terri's questions and Monet's diplomatic manner. So did Tuesdays. Erika's questions provided an empathetic platform for the employees to voice their complaints about unfair treatment.

As Alonzo drove away Tuesday evening, the crew looked forward to Wednesday's plant tour, expecting minimal risk and maximal hospitality, which would be provided by the P.R. person.

Two public relations people greeted the van when Alonzo parked near the security station after the guards opened the gate. A P.R. fellow would help the crew, while Erika would interview the P.R. lady.

Interviewing began close enough to the containment building for the cameras to capture the enormity of the plant. During the outside interview, the P.R. lady used Erika's questions to summarize what the plant did, how many people it employed, and what it contributed to the local economy. Then Erika asked,

"What is the purpose of the containment building?"

"That's where the reactor vats synthesize protein from stem cells. We call it the containment building because any bacteria or viruses that leak from the incubation tanks or reactors stay inside.

Erika's next question prompted a ready reply.

"Do leaks or other accidents happen often?"

"No ma'am. The company has an unblemished safety record.

The P.R. fellow led the crew as the interview continued to the inside plant tour. The roar of the pumps and the throbbing vibrations nearly overpowered Erika's senses, but she and the P.R. lady yelled over the din.

Everyone decompressed when the P.R. fellow took them to the final stop – the enclosed visitors' balcony overlooking the reactor control room.

When helping the crew set the cameras, he said,

"You can point them everywhere except at the window. We let no one take pictures of the control room setup.

The crew positioned cameras that kept Erika and the P.R. lady away from the window. Erika was marching through her questions when a tremor-like vibration swept through, bringing an unplanned question.

"What's that?"

The P.R. fellow answered.

"I don't know, but I'll find out," before dashing into the plant.

Not even the P.R. lady knew what to say until horns started blaring and commands blasted from the public address speaker.

"GO TO THE NEAREST SAFETY AREA AND STAY THERE UNTIL YOU ARE TOLD TO EVACUATE. THIS IS NOT A DRILL I REPEAT, THIS IS NOT A DRILL"

The P.R. lady said,

"We stay here. We're already there.

Not even Erika knew what to say or do. Everyone stood against the window, peering into the control room. Erika stood next to the crew person holding the portable camera and elbowed him in the side. When he turned his head, she silently mouthed,

"Film the control room operators as long as you can.

Erika stared at the operators; they were scrambling about faster and faster as the vibrations intensified until stopping. She glanced at her cell phone before saying,

"I think the vibrations lasted for about–" but the mother of them all struck with a fury that rocked the balcony, smashed the window, and propelled Erika into action.

She screamed,

"We stay here we die. We gotta go," but Alonzo shouted back,

"We can't. They didn't tell us to go.

Erika poked him in the chest before yelling,

"Don't be a fool. Use your head. Everyone, follow me.

Everyone did; As Erika charged into the plant, Alonzo started using his head by taking the rearguard position.

Erika's primal survival instincts kicked in. She took a twisted path to avoid billowing clouds of toxic-looking gas and orange flames emerging from broken pipes and vats, while her brain led them to the van.

Everyone gathered around Erika and Alonzo, gasping for air while waiting for orders.

Erika scanned the scene, trying to find the right words.

"A couple of emergency vans and ambulances are just pulling in. Alonzo, get us back to the motel before someone tries to stop us.

No one spoke until everyone packed their bags and dragged back to the van. Erika and Alonzo did likewise, bringing Terri and Monet.

Terri said,

"Our job's done. We're driving home."

Alonzo found a McDonald's drive-thru two hours later. After everyone had wolfed down enough, Terri said,

"It's amazing how escaping from the jaws of death brings appetites back.

Then she pointed a question at the crew chief.

"Did you bring the video film?"

"I did, and we can add stock footage of a plant blowing up. Erika can add it to the voice-over.

Terri said,

"Here's the plan. Everyone gets tomorrow off but comes to the office on Friday so we can make the final cut that we'll show to Mario on Friday. Hey Alonzo, please plot a course home that stops at your place in DC. I'll drive the rest of us home from there."

Erika retrieved Cassie from Ava's on Thursday afternoon while Terri briefed Mario. The crew finished the final cut by late Friday afternoon. When Terri and Erika showed it to Mario, his excitement bubbled into his voice.

"This can't wait. I'm setting up a Mrs. Harmony conference call right now.

Mrs. Harmony's tone hid her annoyance caused by the six-hour time differential between Manhattan and Brussels. Terri summarized what Mrs. Harmony was viewing but elaborated on the plant disaster.

When finished, Terri said,

"I think we're ready to move on, don't you?"

Mrs. Harmony said,

"Right you are, so why don't –"

Erika's exasperated words barged in.

"Hold on. Don't you think there's gotta be more to the plant blowup? According to the employees we interviewed, there might be a coverup or a conspiracy.

Terri spoke before either boss while glaring at Erika.

"What's with you? Why are you always so paranoid?"

Having heard plenty, Mrs. Harmony ended the meeting.

"Erika's right. Play her angle for a follow-up. You'll have a Labor Day deadline. Make it happen.

Mario disconnected before Terri calmed down enough to say,

"Perhaps Erika's right. We'll just have to see."

"Watching Out and Back"

Terri wanted none of Erika's assistance in developing the follow-up Project Action Plan because she would use the previous one's structure. She would write the script and question list while lining up company P.R. people and willing employees to interview. Alonzo would coordinate logistics and security, and they needed only two recording people to capture Terri and Erika in action – one for the camera and the other for sound recording.

Erika had ample time to work on another class while devoting most of her time to Cassie, whose blossoming accelerated from playing with other children at the mother-daughter meetings.

Seeming particularly energized after an early August session, she asked a question Erika was expecting sooner or later.

"My playmates say doggies are lots of fun. They sleep with them and feed them and clean up any poop they drop. Can I have one?"

Erika kneeled to talk eye-to-eye.

"What kind of doggie would you like?"

"Can we look at some pictures?"

"Sure, we'll do that right after a lunch break."

Cassie sat in the chair next to Erika's, peering into the workstation monitor as Erika described what was scrolling.

"We're looking at photographs of different types of dogs, which are called breeds. We're going through the photographs in alphabetical order. That's like A, B, C, and so on. Please stop me when you see the one you like the most.

Stopping occasionally to name the breed, Erika had been scrolling for fifteen minutes when Cassie yelled,

"Stop momma, stop. That's the one I want.

Erika did before saying,

"Why that's a Scottie. It looks like a loaf of bread covered in shaggy black fur and standing on four stumpy legs. And its cute pointy head has pointy ears sticking out on top. Why don't we see what sort of personality a Scottie has? Personality means what they do and how they behave.

Erika pointed to the words as she read.

"Scottish Terriers are small, compact, short-legged dogs. These characteristics, combined with their intelligence, make them excellent pets when raised from an early age with children and act as a protector on their behalf. Maybe we can find a young one. Let's call a local animal shelter.

Erika did, and after describing what she wanted, the shelter lady said,

"I don't have what you're looking for, but I'll check what other shelters in the area have, and in the meantime, let your daughter browse our selection here. She might find one she likes.

"That's a good way to keep her from being disappointed if she can't get what she wants. I'll bring her in tomorrow.

Cassie did all the talking when Terri poked her head into the kitchen after work.

"Guess where we're going tomorrow? I'm gonna look at dogs and get a pet.

"That's exciting news. I'm sure you'll pick one that'll fit our family. You can tell me more as soon as I change."

After putting Cassie to bed, Erika listened as Terri listed the consequences.

"Aren't we pleasantly busy enough juggling work along with my dating Jocko and your balancing classes and Cassie?"

"Let's not jump the gun. We might not find one she likes.

"OK, but if she does, make sure it can fit in our apartment. I see people walking monstrosities that don't belong in an urban setting.

"Thanks, that's good advice."

The next morning, Erika, accompanied by the shelter lady, wound the stroller through the aisles, talking only when Cassie said something. They had been browsing for twenty minutes when Cassie shouted.

"Stop momma, stop. I want this one.

The shelter lady peered into the cage before explaining Cassie's pick.

"That's a Jack Russell West Highland-Terrior mix. Those in the know call it a Westie-Jack. It looks similar to a Scottie, but I think its tortoiseshell orange and black coloring is prettier than all-black.

This one's gentle and already spayed. And she won't grow much larger. It's a good size for your daughter.

"Does she have a name?"

"We've been calling her Lady because she acts like one, but you can change it.

Cassie poked her fingers through the bars and said,

"Hello, Lady. We're gonna take you home.

Lady's wiggle and tiny whimper showed pure joy.

When Terri came home, Cassie introduced her to the newest family member.

"Hi, Daddy. This is Lady.

Terri played her part, petting Lady's head before saying,

"You have a wonderful owner. I know Cassie's gonna watch out for you.

Erika jumped in by saying,

"And she'll watch out for us. Hey, dinner's on the stove, so why don't you take care of Cassie and Lady while I go to the pet store for supplies?"

"Whatcha gonna get?"

"Taking care of Lady will be almost the same as taking care of Cassie. I'll buy some dog food, a doggie dish and water bowl, and a doggie bed. See you soon."

That night, Terri helped tuck in Cassie and Lady before assessing the family situation. Terri spoke first.

"Looks like you picked the right dog. Let's watch her so she doesn't get pregnant. Our family is now complete – two parents, one child, and one dog. I'm not gonna get pregnant, and I don't think you will either.

"Have you told Jocko?"

"Yep, and in no uncertain terms.

"Excellent. Hey, I don't know about you, but I'm beat. Whatcha say we call it a day?"

"OK, but get ready for Sunday. We depart in three days to start our interview trip."

Using Terri's reminder, Erika called Alonzo the next morning to get the itinerary details. After exchanging typical greetings and telling what she wanted to know, Alonzo happily obliged.

"It's the same as last time only easier because I know the drill. Two days at the same places for employee interviews, and the last day at the same plant with the same P.R. lady.

"Monet's not coming with us this time, but could you put her on the call?"

"Sure, she already knows, but hold on.

Alonzo punched several buttons, and Monet's articulate voice joined in.

"Good morning, Erika. I'm pleased to stay in DC. I've made satisfactory progress on our Ambassadors Project. You and I must hold follow-up meetings with key people soon after you finish Terri's current project.

"I'll be ready. See you then, and Alonzo even sooner."

The itinerary's first two days went even better than Terri had hoped. One of the employees provided x-ray photographs of pipe, pump, reactor, and support welds made by the engineering company that built the plant, showing many were faked.

Terri told Erika to use this fact when interviewing the P.R. lady tomorrow.

The P.R. lady's positive answers deflected Erika's probing questions, but when ending the interview, she asked,

"I have proof obtained at another plant that the construction company repeatedly used the same x-ray photograph for different welds. Would your company be willing to have a regulatory agency examine the welds for the pumps and reactors that blew up here?"

"That decision exceeds my authority. I'll have to ask my superiors.

"That won't be necessary unless I contact you, and until then, I thank you for today's interview.

Erika and the team sat in the van for an hour recapping today's success. Terri complimented Erika's investigative skill, and the crew chief said they had filmed enough to make the final cut a winner.

The guards opened the gate for Alonzo to drive away, but just as he exited, he saw the P.R. fellow from the last time running toward the van, so he rolled down the window to find out what he had to say.

Though out of breath, his ominous words came through loud and clear.

"Don't meddle where you don't belong. It might be dangerous to all of you.

Alonzo said nothing, but as he started driving away, the P.R. fellow ran alongside and yelled,

"Our security guys know how to take care of situations like this. Do you hear me? We'll take care of you.

Alonzo rolled up the window while accelerating, leaving the fellow and his words in the van's wake.

They drove in silence long enough for Terri to consider the implications.

"Gads, that sounds like a threat to all of us." Then she turned to the interview crew and asked,

"Didja get that?"

"It's in the camera.

"Good; Erika. whatcha think?"

"From now on, we'll need Alonzo to watch our back on all projects.

Not even Alonzo said another word regarding the threat, but Terri ended the wrap-up.

"We'll have to hear what the bosses say when we show them the final cut. Hey Alonzo, can you take us to McDonalds?"

"Sure can. I'm hungry too. We'll feel cheerier after eating. Let's forget about the final cut until tomorrow.

Chapter 13
October 2234

"Danger Lurking Everywhere"

A surprise greeted Erika when she and Terri opened the mail on a Saturday in early October. It came in a large envelope from Manhattan Community College. She tried to hide it from her partner, but Terri's reporter instincts prevailed.

"So, what's in there?"

"My diploma and a letter inviting me to the upcoming graduation exercises.

"Gads, I forgot all about your classes. What degree are they awarding you?"

"It's a B.S. in Liberal Arts with a concentration in Creative Writing. It also gives me credit for Big Data and ChatGPT Prompting.

"When is it? I should bring Ava, Ivana, Monet, and Alonzo.

"It doesn't matter. I don't want to go.

"Well how about Ava, Ivana, and I take you for a celebration dinner?"

"Perhaps later, but not now.

"Well, at the very least, Mrs. Harmony should promote you. I've seen Monet in action, so let me handle the negotiations. I'll do that after she tells us what she wants as well as the deadline for our next project.

"When will that be?"

"At Monday's meeting with the bosses. Let me do the talking."

Not even Mario said a word until Mrs. Harmony was about to conclude the meeting.

"You did a fine job on the follow-up plant explosion video, but you've run the legs off additional sequels. Pick up where you left off on up-close-in-person videos showing danger and risk. You need to produce another that lasts for 30 minutes, and your deadline is mid-December. Now, what else do you have?"

Terri said,

"What about the actual threats we got at– "Erika's kick under the table bottled up Terri's words for only a moment until they spilled out with her pained expression.

"What's with you? I'm not gonna shut up.

Mrs. Harmony intervened.

"Erika's right. Drop the plant explosions. Anything else.

Despite a bruised shin, Terri recovered enough to say,

"One other item. You should promote Erika. She just received a degree in Liberal Arts and Creative Writing from Manhattan Community College. How about it?"

"Hmm, no wonder she's such a clever writer. I'll think about it, and while I'm doing that, she can think about your next topic."

Erika had ample free time to work on high-priority projects in both her personal and professional worlds, now that she had graduated. Her personal world would always take precedence, and her daughter would always occupy the top spot.

Cassie's accelerated growth had stabilized at a level that made her more self-sufficient as the months ticked by. She needed less daily supervision because she had support group children, the sound mixer keyboard, and Lady to keep herself occupied. She also had Erika and learned by watching how to use the computer when surfing for information.

Erika also had two professional projects. The Ambassadors project supervised by Monet needed nothing from her at the moment, which meant she could concentrate on Terri's Project Action Plan, which she did for the next several days.

Friday evening, the entire family gathered in the family room. While Cassie and Lady played, Erika surprised Terri by handing three copies of the Action Plan without saying a word while keeping one copy for herself.

**Project Action Plan for Assignment:
Chasing Risks via
Extreme Sports**

Background Information
- **Wealthy Elites and Fitness Addicts want the thrill of defying death.**

- **Sports to Include: Distance runs without protection through African game preserves, Free-Diving in shark-infested waters, Ice Tower Climbing at Niagara Falls, Team Bunge Jumping, Amsterdam's Canal Ice Skating Race.**

Action Plan:
- **Prepare limited Travel Itinerary.**

- **Create thirty-minute video using stock footage for all sports except: Team Bunge Jumping, Ice Tower Climbing, Canal Ice Skating Race (Erika volunteers to demonstrate by participating).**

Who Does What:
- **Terri and Team Researcher provide Background Information.**

- **Film Crew selects Stock Footage.**

- **Terri writes Voice-Over Script and Film Crew edits in Erika's Demonstrations.**

- **Terri hires Alonzo for Itinerary, Logistics, and Security. (He will rent a Hover-Van so Crew can film Erika.}**

———

107

- **Alonzo, Terri, Erika, and one Recording Person who handles both Audio and Video comprise the Travelling Team.**
- **NOTE: EARLY COLD WINTER WEATHER NEEDED FOR ICE TOWER CLIMBING AND CANAL SKATING!**
- **Mario approves final cut and reviews it with Mrs. Harmony by the middle of December.**

Terri needed only a minute to scan its two pages before exclaiming,

"You've nailed everything for everyone, but aren't you a bit presumptuous? You think you can handle bungee jumping and the winter stuff?"

"If this year's winter starts mild, I only need to demo bungee jumping.

"OK, but what's team bungee jumping?"

"I checked the rules, so here they are. A team can have up to five people and a maximum of five jumps. A person can jump at most three times, so if you do the math, a smart team has at least three people if they want to have five jumps.

"Each jump earns points for style, height jumped from, and closest distance to the ground. Greater height and closer distance have more danger, which earns more points, and the team's score equals the sum of its jumps.

"Who's on your team?"

"Just me, unless you or Alonzo want to join.

"Uh, no thanks. I'll ask Alonzo, but I don't think he'll want to risk damaging his Cyber-leg. Where are jumping contests held?"

"That's for you and Alonzo to find.

"OK. Now tell me, what's a hover-van?"

"It's a large aero-car powered by drone-like propellors that move it in all directions. He should know what it is and will like how it gets us up close to the action.

"Mario's gonna love this. Come on, we gotta celebrate with Ava and Ivana your graduation and my project plan. I'm calling them right now to go out on Sunday afternoon."

Terri pushed Cassie's stroller while Erika tugged Lady's leash as they walked to Ava and Ivana's apartment. Lady stayed there while the people went to a nearby family-style restaurant. Its cozy ambiance and large tables made for pleasant conversation that Terri started when directing a question toward Ava.

"How do you like our newest addition to the family?"

"Lady seems nice enough and sure likes Cassie.

Erika jumped in and said,

"Terri and I have an interview trip coming up. Would you be willing to let Cassie and Lady stay? It'll be for only a couple of days.

Ava glanced at Ivana, who looked willing, then answered.

"I guess so. Just make sure you give us the dates and enough dog food.

When Ivana asked about the interview trip, Terri had a ready summary.

"Our video is called 'Chasing Risks via Extreme Endurance Sports'. Many people love the thrill of danger that comes from bungee jumping or climbing Niagara Falls ice towers in winter.

We'll be interviewing thrill seekers in action, and guess what? Erika will join in.

Ivana's scowl came with her words.

"You Americans too foolish. You waste money doing crazy things because country so wealthy, and you want to show off how good you are.

The conversation came to an uncomfortable halt until Erika said,

"You're right, but that's part of human nature. You can find examples throughout history in just about every culture. And I think Americans today do less than before.

Terri found words to segue to another topic.

"Here's a great example of less is more. People across the globe throughout history have always wanted to eat and drink too much, take too many drugs, and have too much sex. But Americans today are cutting back. Why, just look at me and Erika's lifestyles.

Ivana's scowl lessened when she said,

"You told us you gonna date that Jocko guy. You still fooling around?"

Ivana's no-nonsense style nonplussed Terri to the max, so Erika stepped in.

"They're going slow so they get to know one another. Terri says he and a friend want to take Terri and me to a concert sometime. I'll let you know how it goes.

The rest of the conversation brought Cassie into the spotlight, and by the time the group trooped back to the apartment, any unpleasantness had been left behind.

Erika had all her professional projects taken care of, which meant she could devote her time to caring for Cassie and surfing the web while simply waiting for Terri and Alonzo to launch the travel itinerary. That's precisely what she was doing when Terri called her at lunchtime on October 31st. After she said hello, Terri took control.

"Guess what, sport? Alonzo just found a bungee jumping contest that's tailor-made for us. It'll take place at noon on Veteran's Day next to the Washington Monument. Events DC is sponsoring it, and National Park Service rangers will run it. It'll set up the jumping tower, and the contest should be safe enough because rangers will put the jumper in a safety harness.

"And I've saved the best for last. Alonzo got permission to enter you as a one-person team and hover near enough to film everything. How do you like that?"

Erika could feel lunch starting to stir but didn't let it come up in her words.

"I guess I better start practicing. Maybe Jocko can give me some pointers.

Terri's concern showed in her voice.

"You mean you haven't done anything yet? OK, I'll get you lined up with Jocko. Bye-bye."

Jocko came through the following week, giving her enough training and a jumper's uniform to look like she knew what she was doing. By the time Alonzo drove the crew before dawn's earliest light on the 11th, Erika felt calm enough to joke about Terri's call.

"I thought she was playing a Halloween trick, but thanks to Jocko and Alonzo, perhaps it'll be a first-time treat for me."

Erika listened for the rest of the drive as the team reviewed procedures.

Events DC must have done a thorough P.R. job because an expectant throng surrounded the monument just far enough away to stay clear of the jumpers. Just before Erika joined the jumpers responding to the official's call, Terri asked,

"How many jumps are you gonna make?"

"I don't know; you'll have to watch; I hope I look OK for the camera.

Erika dashed away. Alonzo took the team to the hover-van.

The camera person planned to film the entire three-hour contest and record whatever up-close comments Terri would make.

"This is Terri Tarrant reporting from the first team bungee jumping competition ever held near the Washington Monument. Let me summarize the rules…"

Terri made intermittent comments that would keep the viewers engaged but added more details when Erika was on the platform.

"And here's IBN's very own Erika Kincaid. She's never bungee-jumped before but volunteered to show and tell the action. She's wearing earbuds and a microphone so we can have a two-way conversation. Erika, how does it feel?"

"Like I'm swaying in the wind, which I am. It's gusty up here, but here I GOOO…"

Her swan dive looked as good as many competitors, and she spoke again when her turn for the second dive came up.

"The jolt I get at the bottom is thrilling. What an endorphin rush. I'm gonna try tumbling this time. BYE-BYEEE…"

Terri yelled,

"Look at her go…she's using her high school cheerleading skills… bravo.

Erika surprised even Alonzo when getting set for a third jump.

"Now I understand why jumpers wanna go to the edge. I'm gonna try jumping backwards and spinning on the way DOOWWNNN…"

But a gust of wind surprised her, turning her into an out-of-control pendulum that bounced into the Monument. The ranger manning the safety harness rope pulled her lifeless body slowly to the ground and into the awaiting arms of the EMTs.

Terri held it together long enough to end the video.

"I have to see how my partner is. This is Terri Tarrant signing off.

Terri raced to the medical tent as soon as the hover-van landed. Alonzo and the recording person followed but waited at the entrance. Spotting the doctor in charge, she walked to her, stopping before saying,

"I'm Terri Tarrant of IBN. I think your EMTs are examining a member of my team. Do you know how she is?"

"Let's take a look. Follow me.

The tent's uncrowded condition let them stand close to the examining table. Terri listened as the doctor explained what was going on.

"They've got her sitting up. She's conscious; that's a good sign. Now they'll ask if she knows who and where she is and why they're examining her.

The doctor continued as soon as Erika answered correctly.

"Now, they'll check for bruises, broken bones, and a concussion. She might have one because she hit the wall pretty hard.

The doctor moved next to the EMT who was checking for that. Five minutes later, he turned to the doctor.

"She has a concussion but is stable enough to go home. She'll be achey tomorrow when the adrenaline rush wears off. Someone should look after her for a day or two to make sure the symptoms go away.

Terri blurted,

"I'll do that. What should I look for?"

"Headache of course, but also dizziness, nausea, and sensitivity to light.

"OK, can I talk to her?"

"Sure, but don't hug or pull on her.

Terri moved right in front.

"You scared us all to death. How do you feel?"

Her answer was stronger than her wan smile.

"Like I've been gang-tackled a hundred times by the winning Superbowl team, but at least I'm alive.

She pulled herself up when she saw the rest of her team coming in, then had the presence of mind to say,

"Why don't you have the camera record you interviewing the doctor with me standing next to her? The viewers will wanna see my condition after I slammed into the Washington Monument.

Hearing her words, Alonzo said,

"Everyone stay here. I'll get the recording gear."

Starting the drive home half an hour later, Alonzo asked,

"Should we stop for something to eat?"

Erika gave the answer.

"I'm famished. Nerves kept me from eating much for breakfast, and I skipped lunch, so please take us to a McDonalds."

Erika needed to rest on most of the drive home. While her team recapped the day and planned for tomorrow, Erika mused in privacy.

Today's excitement knocked more sense into me. I'm not as fit as I need to be, and I have to pay more attention when I'm in dangerous places. If I'm not too stiff and sore, I'll start tomorrow.

Chapter 14
December 2234

"Packing for Protection"

When Erika realized she needed two recovery days at home alone to regain her step, Terri called Ava, explaining why Cassie and Lady should remain with her until Erika felt better. Ava agreed, and Terri went to the office so she and a video editor could complete the final cut.

Erika felt good enough on Friday morning to join Terri for previewing the final cut with Mario. Terri had already briefed him about Erika's collision, which explained why he looked at her when starting the meeting.

"No doubt about it. I'll tell Mrs. Harmony you've earned a promotion if she doesn't say the same when we meet with her."

Erika deflected the praise by saying,

"Let's see my performance in the final cut.

Terri did all the talking to the end. Then Mario said,

"It's early enough to call Mrs. Harmony. I'm setting up an online conference call right now.

Both Mario and Terri talked Mrs. Harmony through the final cut. When finished, everyone waited for her decision.

"This is the most viewer-gripping video IBN has ever produced. Erika's gutsy jumping and Terri's ability to stifle her emotions while showing Erika emerging from the medical tent almost choked me up. Mario, promote both of them. I see that Erika's sitting with you and Terri, but when will she be ready to return full-time?"

Erika spoke right up.

"Thank you, Mrs. Harmony, for promoting both of us. How about giving Terri an early February deadline for our next assignment? I'll use the time off in December to help develop the Project Action Plan.

"You've got it, and Terri, make sure you hire Alonzo on every project. Any final comments?"

None came, so Mrs. Harmony ended the call.

Mario was the first to talk afterward.

"Terri, what's your plan for December?"

"I'll come to the office, network with the crew, and keep Alonzo in the loop. Why don't we conference-call him right now and share all the good news?"

Half an hour later, after hearing from Mario and Terri, Alonzo shared additional information.

"Just for the heck of it, I checked on what happened at the Niagara Falls ice tower climb and the Amsterdam canal race. And guess what? Bad weather hit both. The ice towers were too soft to climb, and a freak storm plus a subsea earthquake in the North Sea sent a tsunami-like wave crashing into the canals close to shore, cracking the ice and drowning some spectators. Erika's collision kept us from getting into more danger.

Terri made the last comment.

"OK, then I'm promoting you by adding weather monitoring to your logistics and security services. That way, we'll pack the right gear no matter the weather. And don't worry; I'll give you a pay raise too."

Erika chose drafting Terri's action plan as the starting point on her road to complete recovery, for it would be the least demanding physically and give both her and Terri the most personal time for the rest of the year. She didn't tell her, but instead wrapped four copies to make an early Christmas present she placed on the kitchen table at breakfast the following Saturday. She also placed two for Cassie.

Terri followed Erika's orders and opened hers first. Happiness showed when she spoke after skimming the Plan.

Project Action Plan for Assignment: The Post-Modern Approach to Fitness

Background Information
- **Men and Women, but especially Women want to feel good and look good.**
- **Overindulgence in Food, Drink, Drugs, and Sex is part of Human Nature.**
- **Trends in Nutrition.**
- **Trends in Drug Usage.**
- **Trends in Cosmetics.**

Action Plan:
- **Interviews only in New York City.**
- **Create thirty-minute video using stock footage**

Who Does What:
- **Terri and Team Researcher provide Background Information.**
- **Film Crew selects Stock Footage.**
- **Terri writes Voice-Over Script and Film Crew edits in Terri's interviews at Rehab Clinic, with Nutrition Counselor, with Fitness Trainer, and Cosmetician.**
- **Terri hires Alonzo for Itinerary, Logistics, and Security.**
- **Erika demonstrates Fitness Routines and Cosmetician Treatment.**
- **Mario approves final cut and reviews it with Mrs. Harmony by the middle of February.**

"This gift's at the top of my Santa's wish list. It gives me more cruising time to handle my stuff, while your demos fit nicely into your recovery plan.

"I thought you'd like it. Hey, why don't you help Cassie open her presents?"

Terri let Cassie unwrap the first, then said,

"Goodness, look at this. It's a children's picture book called 'The First Christmas Night'. You'll learn all about the birth of baby Jesus. Now let's see what's in the other.

After Cassie did so, Terri spoke again.

"And this is a book called 'Santa's Story'. Golly, you'll know more about the meaning of Christmas than most of your playmates when we finish reading them."

"OK, you two. We'll do some reading after everyone eats their oatmeal, so please dig in."

While Terri started implementing her part of the plan at the office the following week, Erika worked out at the health club, putting Cassie in its daycare room. When Jocko saw her using a weight machine, he trotted over.

"Looks like you're starting a New Year's resolution early. Can I give you some more tips?"

"Please do. The pointers you gave me earlier worked fine.

When finished a half-hour later, Jocko gave another.

"I was gonna call Terri, but telling you first is even better. How about you and Terri come to a New Year's Eve dance party with me and a buddy other than Jimmy?"

"OK, but call Terri. She'll give the final word and tell you where to pick us up.

"That's a deal.

"Well thank you. We could talk more but I need to get Cassie, so bye-bye until New Year's Eve."

Erika told Terri at supper that night. She liked the idea.

"How nice. And how about they pick us up at Ava's, so we can leave Cassie there? Lady should be OK staying home because we'll be gone less than a day.

"Excellent plan. Everything's fitting in."

Erika found something else to fit in a couple of days before Christmas: another mother-daughter care group meeting. During the break, one of the mothers came to Erika.

"Whatever you're doing for your daughter, keep doing it. She's developing so quickly.

"Thank you for the compliment. We're both having lots of fun doing things together.

Seeing Erika's pleased look, the mother said more.

"I think she's big enough to enjoy the Saint Luke's Christmas Eve Pageant Service. It's held every year. It'll add to her understanding if she already knows the story, and give her something new if she doesn't.

"That's a terrific recommendation. Thank you so much. We're gonna do it."

Terri loved it and arranged for ridesharing to and from. After coming home and putting Cassie to bed, the duo reminisced in the family room.

"I will always treasure the memories of my parents taking me to those magical Christmas Eve services from the early years. The decorated trees, soft lighting, and joyful singing are part of me. How about you?"

"I don't have that, but you and Cassie are helping make new ones. Terri asked,

"Have you recovered enough for me to give you a Christmas Eve hug?"

Erika answered by showing.

The days between Christmas and New Year's Eve melted away for the duo. Cassi liked the excitement of everything they did for her, especially staying at Ava's. Jocko and his buddy whisked them away at 7:30 to the dance party.

Erika liked her date, a good-looking fitness trainer named Nick who talked and danced as good as he looked. During one of their beverage breaks, Jocko surprised her when he started comparing the music featured at the party.

"I like music played by both an orchestra and a rock group, but the classical pieces from the past beat the contemporary stuff pushed on us today.

Erika listened to comments coming from the others, especially from Terri.

"You might be right. Erika and I plan to take an online music appreciation class in the New Year. We can talk more about it after I know more.

Jocko didn't get a chance to reply, because Nick said,

"The rock groups powering up. Let's it get on with more dancing.

The foursome counted down to Midnight and then sang Auld Lange Syne with the crowd before sipping champagne. Erika nudged Terri and pointed to her cell phone, hinting they should leave.

Terri smiled expectantly as she said,

"Good idea, but I'm not ready to end the excitement. We'll drop you off at home, but I'm spending the night with Jocko.

Erika pursed and popped her lips before saying,

"OK, but be careful.

Terri tapped her purse and said,

"Not to worry. I'm packing protection, just in case."

Terri and Erika returned fully re-energized to the office on the first Monday after New Year's Eve, diving into recording the next video. Alonzo said it was Terri's easiest assignment for him. Jocko agreed to let the camera person record training Erika, and a local cosmetician liked the publicity the video would generate from glamorizing her.

The team finished filming during the last week of January, giving Terri and the video editor two weeks to complete the final cut and Erika time off until participating in Mario's review meeting.

Erika used early February's longer days and unseasonably mild temperatures to take Cassie out in the stroller. The first Saturday in February's weather looked promising as Erika packed up, put Cassie in the stroller, and started pushing along streets in a nearby blue-collar neighborhood.

The early morning street and sidewalk traffic were nil, allowing Erika to gaze at the storefronts she passed without worrying about cars or people.

But that changed abruptly not more than fifteen seconds after crossing a street-lighted intersection. She heard screeching tires and a racing engine coming from behind. She halted against a storefront just in time to see the driver's side of a black sedan whoosh by, slowing just enough for someone to open the rear door and fling a brief-case onto the pavement before the driver burned rubber to escape.

Erika didn't move, but suddenly, her brain elevated to a higher state, giving a clearer picture of the situation.

That must be a drug dealer ditching his stash before the cops catch him. Where are they? They must be close behind.

Fifteen seconds later, squealing tires, a wailing siren, and flashing blue lights said she was right. She waited long enough for the siren to fade before taking action.

As the only person to see where the briefcase had ended up, she retrieved it from underneath a parked car, then put it on the stroller's carrying shelf and pushed in the original direction, pretending nothing had happened.

She walked for twenty minutes before retracing her steps, calming down for the moment but keeping her awareness elevated. Doing so paid off when she saw the dealer's car creeping toward her. She stood against a storefront and faced the street, preparing to act.

Stopping next to her in the wrong lane, a fellow climbed out from the rear seat before saying,

"Hey lady, didja see a briefcase on the pavement? I lost mine and it would sure be a big help if you—" His words stuck in his throat when Erika showed it before saying,

"And I already checked it out, so I know it's loaded with neatly packed plastic bags containing dope. You're the local mafioso boss working the streets in this neighborhood. What's your name?"

He regained enough of his wits to reply.

"Look, lady, don't get cute with me or I'll smack ya before grabbing my stuff and—" This time, his words froze when Erika pulled the Glock from her bag before saying,

"Tell your driver to stand beside you before I put a bullet through the window. Do it now." Five seconds later, two guys who looked like they stepped out of a gangster movie faced her.

"So, what are your names?"

The driver looked at the rear seat guy, who had no option other than answering.

"Du-dey call me Vincenzo; mu-my driver's Bosco. Hu-how come you pack-en a Glock?"

"I don't trust anyone, so here's the deal. I'm not gonna give your stash to the cops; they might try to sell it. I'm not gonna keep it, because I don't wanna try either. That leaves only one option; I'll give it back."

"Bu-but why?"

"Look, I don't judge anyone. You're selling dope to people who want it. If you didn't, they'd buy it somewhere else, probably for a higher price, and they might hurt someone to get the money. And selling drugs at least gives you and your gang something to do for the time being. So, take it and go before somebody notices."

Vincenzo grabbed it before saying,

"Lady, we got our own code of honor. I owe you big time. You gimme your name; I'll give ya my number, and ya call me if ya need help. I ain't as stupid as ya think. I know what's goin' on.

"My name's Erika Kincaid, and Cassandra's my daughter. What's your number?"

Erika repeated it after he rattled it off, then ended by saying,

"I know what's going on too, but for some things, not as much as you. Thanks for backing me up if I need help.

"Ya got it Erika. Keep it secret."

Her humor returned with her smile.

"Now that's a deal we both can live with. You be careful, and I will too."

Chapter 15
March 2235

"Testing More Than the Water"

Erika let her encounter with Vincenzo fade into the background soon after returning to work the following week. Terri told her that Mario wanted to hold the final cut review Friday morning and would conference-connect Mrs. Harmony if he liked what he saw.

Erika knew he would but waited for him to say so, which he did after Terri summarized what he was seeing.

"This is better than good. Erika's becoming quite a performer, looking good in the gym and the beauty salon. Let's get Mrs. Harmony's judgment.

Mario intended to play the entire video, letting Terri narrate, but Mrs. Harmony called a halt after fifteen minutes.

"No wonder the media research shows our ratings going up. Erika's got the looks and the words, nearly matching Terri's. Keep it up.

Terri felt a tinge of jealousy but concealed it, instead saying,

"We will. What do you want to see next, and when?"

"Find something that connects to the Superpower battles and power grabs you did. It'll be a change of pace from the current ones. Get the final cut done by mid-May. I think that should be achievable.

Terri avoided looking at Erika, simply saying,

"We'll do it," before Mrs. Harmony ended the meeting.

Erika detected Terri's miffed feelings but let it slide.

"Mrs. Harmony likes how you put the final cut together. Why don't I draft our next action plan by working at home while you stay here and keep the crew happy?"

"Go ahead. I'll see you later."

Erika noticed that Terri kept her distance when at home but didn't make an issue of it. She kept busy with Cassie while working on the action plan. Nothing useful came to mind, but she mused while watching Cassie play with Lady.

They sure have their own way of playing. They're not fighting; they're just having fun. What were those videos Mrs. Harmony mentioned? I got it, The Superpowers Battle for The Poles and

The Superpowers Battle for Indigenous People. Hmm.

Something Vincenzo said just flashed, code of ethics. Another name for it is Honor among Thieves. Lemme try to connect all this.

The connection came when Erika awoke in the middle of the night.

I've got it. Our video will show how we sometimes can't trust the people in power we're supposed to. I'm gonna write the plan while the words are flowing in my head.

Erika worked in splendid silence for three hours before printing four copies.

Project Action Plan for Assignment:
The Great American Power Grab

Background Information
Different Groups want "Power Over the People", not "Power to the People".
- **Big Government Agencies lie to frighten People (I.R.S.)**
- **Big Healthcare does likewise so People use their services.**
- **Big Businesses entice People to buy more than they need.**
- **Foreign Countries scam People to get their data.**

Action Plan:
- **Interviews only in New York City.**
- **Create thirty-minute video using stock footage**

Who Does What:
- **Terri and Team Researcher provide Background Information.**
- **Film Crew selects Stock Footage.**
- **Terri writes Voice-Over Script and Film Crew edits in Terri's interviews of Erika at selected locations (I.R.S. Office, Doctor's Office, Health Foods Store)**
- **Terri hires Alonzo for Itinerary, Logistics, and Security.**
- **Erika poses as a typical citizen.**
- **Mario approves final cut and reviews it with Mrs. Harmony by the middle of May.**

She read it three times before a last thought came to mind.
Terri should like this, but I won't show her until she warms up to Cassie and me. I have lots to do before then.

Erika used Terri's time away to bring Cassie with her on a mid-week visit to Alonzo and Monet in DC, leaving a note before Terri awoke. They arrived in time for a snack that Monet had just prepared.

While Monet entertained Cassie, Erika showed Alonzo the action plan. He studied it for only a few minutes before saying,

"You're making my job easier and easier, but I'll make sure Terri gets her money's worth. I'm sure she'll like it.

"You're the only person who's seen it. Don't mention it until she does.

"Is there something going on with her?"

"I think she's jealous because the bosses said my looks and words are catching up to hers.

Alonzo rubbed the back of his neck while twisting his head from side to side before saying,

"She'll get over it; just give her more time.

"I will."

Cassie took a nap while the three adults talked about the Ambassadors Project. Monet led the discussion.

After reviewing what she had done since Erika's last briefing, she said,

"We must test the water before introducing our project to appropriate nations. My counterparts at the NAIA and IPWA like what we are proposing but are concerned about your assisting me. They assume that your reporting job will bias our recommendations. That's why I will schedule a meeting as soon as you are ready to help state our case. I recommend late May.

Erika poked Alonzo before saying,

"May works for me if it works for both of you.

Alonzo's words ended the conversation.

"I'm ready whenever you ladies say it's time. And it's time for me to get you back to Union Station, unless you want to spend the night here.

"Thanks, but if we leave now, we'll be home by midnight, and Cassie can nap on the train.

"OK, then let's go."

Terri didn't miss Erika or Cassie when she rushed home from work after stopping at a drugstore. She wanted no one present when administering the test.

She literally ripped off her clothes before opening the test kit and whipping out the instructions. Then she tried to calm down enough so she could urinate into a cup. It took a half hour, but that gave her enough time to read the pregnancy testing details.

The kit contains two test strips. They detect the pregnancy hormone hCG. I missed two periods, but that's happened before, and I don't have nausea or swollen breasts. It takes only three minutes after dipping the strip into urine for it to change color. If the color above the test line turns pink, I'm ninety-nine percent certain I'm pregnant.

Terri steadied the cup on the bathroom sink before dipping the stick and looking away, as she thought about the consequences.

What'll this do to my career? What about my life with Erika? And what about Jocko? Time's up; let's look at the results.

Terri saw pink, panicked; and screamed at the strip.

"You're lying. This is impossible. I'm not on the pill and don't have an IUD, but Jocko and I take great care in bed. What am I gonna do?"

Terri threw the cup and strip away. Then she put the instructions back in the kit before hiding it in the bottom drawer of her bathroom's storage cabinet before making a pledge.

I'll wait a week and use the other strip. And if I'm pregnant, I still have options. I tell no one until I have to.

Chapter 16
May 2235

"Oh No! Grab and Go"

Although Erika and Terri continued working apart, which seemed to work out well for both of them, Erika did make an unannounced trip to the office, planning to meet briefly with Mario.

Glancing around, she didn't see Terri, so she marched into his office; when he heard her come in, he abruptly ended the phone call before saying,

"We're not holding the final cut review today. Why are you here?"

"To tell you I don't need to attend. I know you and Mrs. Harmony will love it. The script and questions Terri wrote made it so easy for me, she should get all the credit.

"Don't you wanna see your performance?"

"Look, I was there. I don't need you to tell me I'm looking good. Noticing her no-nonsense expression, Mario replied,

"OK, don't get huffy. Have you told her?"

"No. you can if she asks.

"That'll work."

"And tell her to tell me what Mrs. Harmony says about a topic and completion date for the next assignment."

"Will do. When'll you be back?"

"When Terri shows you the next Project Action Plan, which I'll be thinking about between now and then."

When Terri came home early two weeks later, Erika knew why but played along while she watched Cassie and Lady wrestle.

"The bosses love our latest video. Mario told me you told him I should get all the credit because the script and questions I gave you made your interviews easy. Maybe so, but you're the one that pulled them off. You were great.

Erika came toward Terri, then stopped before saying,

"We're a team. I help you and you help me.

Terri burst into tears, and Erika hugged her, saying nothing.

When the tears subsided, Terri choked out,

"I'm sorry for being jealous. It'll never happen again.

Erika's words and smile carried over to Terri.

"I've already been thinking about the next assignment and its completion date. Why don't you tell us at supper what Mrs. Harmony said?"

"I'm famished. Let's eat early.

Terri hurried away to change clothes. Erika scooted to the kitchen.

When Terri said she's getting bigger and bigger and helping train Lady, Cassie giggled before saying,

"Oh yes, I am. Momma says you were busy. That's where you were. Can we play sometime?"

"How about right after supper? You pick the game and we'll play.

"Momma, I'm full. Can I go?"

"Yes, you're excused."

When Cassie scampered away, Erika asked,

"So, what did Mrs. Harmony say?"

"She's leaving it up to us to pick the topic, and we've got a mid-July deadline.

"I like mid-July. Why don't I draft the plan and you tell Mario he'll have something to look at in a couple of weeks?"

Terri got up to go before saying,

"I like that too."

Feeling even more energetic now that she and Terri were copacetic again, Erika spent most of the next morning thinking about project topics she had always wanted to cover but would also build on the last one.

She took a break after lunch to play with Cassie, and when she returned to her project plan ruminations, the plan leaped into focus.

She finished it an hour later but needed to call a recent contact to confirm her part. She had written down his number after their first meeting, but she recalled it from memory. Vincenzo answered on the fifth ring.

"You called. Whatcha want?"

"This is Erika Kincaid. Do you remember me?"

Vincenzo didn't skip a beat.

"The Glock lady. Ya need help?"

"It's more like I need you to do something that'll help both of us. Does that sound interesting?"

"Sorta. Say more.

"My partner, Terri Tarrant, and I make videos shown on networks worldwide for International Breaking News. I would like to interview you, one of your lieutenants, and one of your street dealers to show the viewers that –" Vincenzo's yelling cut her off.

"You nuts? All da public wanna see is us getting nabbed by the cops.

Erika yelled back before he could say more.

"Just listen to me. I'm gonna show that your local gang is smarter than people think, and my partner's gonna show that some of the so-called smart people in government agencies aren't so smart. Of course, I won't mention names, and my camera crew will blur faces and mask voices. We'll do the interviews wherever you choose, and I won't release the video until you approve it. And I'll pay you and your lieutenants or enforcers for doing it. Whatcha say?"

Vincenzo spoke thirty seconds later.

"OK, and it won't cost. Some P.R. can't hurt. When d'ya wanna do it?"

"How does the first or second week in June sound?"

"OK.

"How much lead time will you need?"

"Nada. You call me, I call two of my guys, and we get where we tell ya ipso pronto.

"Thanks, I'll call you soon.

Erika needed another break, so she and Cassie went to the kitchen for juice and cookies. After that, she printed four copies of the plan, skimmed it once, and made plans to show it to Terri that evening.

Project Action Plan for Assignment: Smart People, Not-So-Smart People, and the Mafia

Background Information
The Public's Misconceptions about the Intelligence and Common Sense of Different Groups need to be corrected.
- **"Smart People": DOD and NASA, Military Planners, International Security Advisors, University Presidents**

- **"Not-So-Smart People": Newscasters, Sanitation Engineers, Construction Workers**

- **"The Mafia": The Boss, Lieutenants, Street Dealers**

Action Plan:
- **Conduct In-Person Interviews.**

- **Create thirty-minute video using only the Interviews.**

Who Does What:
- **Terri and Team Researcher provide Background Information for Terri's interviews.**

- **Terri writes Voice-Over Script and lines up Smart and Dumb People for the Interviews she conducts.**

- **Erika provides Background Information foe her interviews.**

- **Erika writes Voice-Over Script and lines up Mafia People for the Interviews she conducts.**

———

131

- **Alonzo coordinates Itinerary and provides Logistics and Security Services.**
- **Mario approves final cut and reviews it with Mrs. Harmony by mid-July.**

When the duo settled in the family room after tucking Cassie in, Erika handed Terri the plan and told her to skim it.

She did for a minute before saying,

"I think I know what you're getting at, but explain it to me.

"Think about it this way. Just about everyone has preconceived notions about who's good and who's not, and who's smart and who's not. Let's give the viewers new insights. If you handle the smart and not-so-smart people interviews, their words will show the smart ones aren't so smart, and the not-so-smart ones know more than we give them credit if you lead the interview with the right questions.

"OK, now I see it. That's clever, but what are the mafia interviews supposed to show?"

"I'll ask questions that might let the viewers see a different side. In all cases, we're not judging. We'll let the viewers do that."

"But geez Louise, how will you find the right mafioso?"

"Trust me. I'm clever and resilient."

Terri now spent as much time as possible with Erika and Cassie. She seemed almost back to normal, but Erika noticed that during quiet times, she would occasionally stare into space while interlocking her fingers. Her forlorn look pinged Erika's empathy, but she forced herself not to pry.

She looks like she's praying for deliverance from something on her mind. Is it my imagination, or is there some problem she's keeping to herself? Maybe something will happen that will make her tell me.

But nothing did, so Erika bided her time.

Erika kept busy on all fronts, especially with Cassie, and she took advantage of late June's pleasant weather by taking her for evening strolls in the stroller. She had several routes; her favorite ended on a one-way street going her way where cars had to turn to the right before doubling back on a parallel road only a quarter of a block away. The storefront shops closed at six, which kept night-time traffic to nil.

She took that route on June 21st, the longest day of the year, and told Cassie about it as they strolled. They were near the turnaround point when she said,

"It's dark now at about 9:30, but the sun didn't set until 9. It's so nice to have—" Erika's words couldn't come out because a pair of strong hands grabbed her shoulders from behind and threw her to the pavement. Her head hitting first stunned her. She couldn't see but could only hear what happened next.

"Momma, help, help," followed by the sounds of a door slamming and a car racing away.

Cassie's scream cleared Erika's brain, putting her back in action.

She grabbed her Glock and raced after the car, thinking as she ran.

No one's gonna grab my daughter. I know where the car's going and I can get there first.

She ran to the alley that intersected her street and then flew across to the parallel road. The sounds of a car skidding around the corner and speeding her way said she was right.

She blasted bullets into the passenger's side front and rear tires, bringing it to a swerving halt on the sidewalk. Then she shattered the rear door window with another before sticking her head in to see who was where: Cassie crying in the front seat next to a guy stuck behind the steering wheel.

Erika's final bullet needed no words. Then she grabbed Cassie and streaked back the way she came before kissing Cassie to calm her, then putting her and the Glock back in the stroller and hurrying toward home while calming down enough to think.

No one saw me or the action… I'm in the clear, and the snatcher will never talk. Nor will I. I'll leave that for the police.

Did I commit a crime? No, I did what I had to for Cassie's sake. Every mother would do the same. And when we get home, I'll tell her tonight's excitement is our secret, never to be shared with anyone. And whenever I'm out, I must keep my laptop, cell phone, and Glock close by.

Erika stayed in the shadows all the way home.

Chapter 17
July 2235

"A Secret No Longer"

Vincenzo OK'd Erika's interviews, which meant video editing could begin. Alonzo said she did a masterful job bridging the gap between his gang and what people think of the mafia. He also said Terri lacked energy, which explained why she missed the deadline by a few days. Mario didn't mind because the Fourth of July celebration would distract viewers' attention until the combined interview videos aired.

Terri insisted Erika attend the final cut meeting in case the bosses asked questions she couldn't handle, but that didn't happen, so everyone came away happy, particularly the duo because Mrs. Harmony gave them a Halloween completion date for the next project. They decided to postpone working on it until the start of August.

Terri's energy level recovered some, but not to what Erika expected. Still, she waited for something that would reveal the reason. She and Terri were sitting in the kitchen, sipping drinks after supper, when Cassie hopped in, carrying what looked like a folded instruction brochure.

Handing it to Erika, she said,

"Look what I found in Daddy's bathroom. Can you read it to me?"

"Sure, let's see what it is.

Erika dropped the Coke but kept from spilling it before disguising her fib.

"Oh, it's nothing important. Why don't you go play with Lady? We'll be there soon.

Erika handed it to Terri as soon as Cassie hopped away.

"Why do you have pregnancy test kit instructions?"

Terri's embarrassed flush answered before her words.

"Because I'm pregnant.

Erika hid her shocked reaction but shouted to herself.

That's why she has no energy, even though she snacks all the time. I won't say anything until I hear from her.

Erika won the waiting game. Terri spoke a minute later.

"I've known since March. I can't get a grip on what to do. What do you think?"

"Have you told Jocko?"

"Not yet, but I have to before my baby bump shows.

"Have you talked about what might happen if you get pregnant?"

"Not really. He says he loves me, but we're spending less time in bed because I'm too tired most of the time. I don't see him as often, which might tell me he's looking around.

Her brain suddenly snapping into action, Erika straightened her shoulders and took command.

"It's too soon to visit an ob-gyn, but let's get you to a pregnancy counselor. I'll get a recommendation from my mother-daughter support group. Why don't you go play with Cassie while I do?"

When Terri came back an hour later, Erika told her the next step.

"I've set up an appointment for next Tuesday morning with a perinatal psychiatrist. Her office is in the Mount Sinai Children's Hospital medical building. That's where Cassie's pediatrician is."

Terri rebounded enough to say,

"Good thing we're on a work break. Let's ride-share to get there and back.

"We will, and please let your mind take a break from thinking about what we'll do after that. The shrink might give us some good advice."

———

Terri followed enough of Erika's advice to show a better attitude when meeting the psychiatrist. Cassie waited nearby when the doctor started the meeting.

"Good morning. I am Doctor Wilma Custer. Which of you is Erika Kincaid?"

Erika leaned forward after nodding.

"I made the appointment for my partner, Marilyn Tarrant. Terri, why don't you take it from here?"

Terri talked for twenty minutes, giving all the information she had and answering Doctor Custer's questions that came along the way. When Terri finished, the doctor continued.

"Half my load is for the perinatal period with patients whose situations are like yours. Thirty percent of pregnant women seek counseling. The other half is for the postpartum period, where fifteen percent need help.

The doctor paused for questions. When none came, she said more.

"You've expressed all the concerns about careers, marriage, and the impact on relationships with people other than the father. You must decide if you want to end the pregnancy or continue to delivery. If you choose to end it, you have options, but all of them need guidance from a medical professional. It is illegal any other way.

Terri's frown prompted Erika to step in.

"Do you have any pamphlets telling us more?"

"I have two that may help. The first explains abortion options, and the second gives commonsense rules for living, no matter the situation. After you discuss them, please call if you would like to schedule another session.

Erika took two of each to make their discussion easier, which Terri said they'd do that night.

The partners sat at the kitchen table after Cassie fell asleep, Terri talking first.

"I picked the kitchen in case a case of the munchies overpowers me. How about I tackle the abortion pamphlet and you take the rules for living?"

"OK, but we can skip yours if you can answer this question – do you want to have a child?"

"I'm struggling with it.

Erika jumped in to add some assurance.

"It certainly will affect your career and lifestyle, and it will impact your relationship with Jocko, but it won't affect ours. Go ahead with abortion info.

Terri kept thumbing through it while talking.

"There are two types, the abortion pill and the in-clinic procedure. Pills might contain either mifepristone or misoprostol, and both can cause cramping or bleeding. It doesn't tell if an overdose can kill you, but the tongue-twisting side effects sound frightening. I better move on to the in-clinic type.

Terri grimaced when she proceeded.

"There's the suction aspiration method that vacuums-out the uterus. Then there's the D and C that removes tissue inside it.

She shuddered before saying,

"I'm stopping here before what it says does more than remove my appetite. You go on with the rules of living stuff.

Having already glanced through it, Erika said,

"Turn to the 'Guidelines for Living Smart' page."

GUIDELINES FOR LIVING SMART

MEMORIZE THIS LIST:
1. **ACCEPT IMPERFECTION.**

    NO ONE CAN GET THINGS RIGHT ALL THE TIME.

2. **SHARE YOUR VULNERABILITY.**

    EVERYONE EXPERIENCES OCCASIONAL EMOTIONAL WEAKNESSES.

3. **KNOW WHAT UPSETS YOU.**

    EVERYONE HAS IRRATIONAL FEARS.

4. **ACCEPT WHAT YOU FIND DIFFICULT.**

EVERYONE STRUGGLES WITH SOMETHING FROM TIME TO TIME.

5. **REWARD YOURSELF FOR BEING GOOD ENOUGH.**

    YOU DON'T HAVE TO BE NUMBER ONE ALL THE TIME.

6. **OVERCOME ROMANTICISM.**

    INFATUATION SOON FADES. NO ONE WILL MAKE YOU HAPPY ALL THE TIME.

7. **DESPAIR CHEERFULLY.**

    DEAL WITH GLOOMY TIMES AND SETBACKS PROACTIVELY.

8. **TRANSCEND YOURSELF.**

    REALIZE THAT THE UNIVERSE IS FAR GREATER THAN EVERYONE.

She waited for Terri before continuing.

"They're all self-explanatory, and two in particular apply to you. Take a look at number three. If you haven't made up your mind about having a baby, you should choose the lesser of two fears – having an abortion or having a baby. No one can make that choice but you. Number six is the other. You'll have to talk that one out with Jocko.

"You're right, and I won't wait for him to call. I'll set something up tomorrow. I'm no longer hungry, but I am tired. Let's go to bed."

Terri went to the health club after lunch the next day. Spotting Jocko coaching another female, she walked to the weight machine and waited for him to notice.

When he did, he told his trainee to take a break before saying,

"You haven't been here for a while. What's up?"

"I'll tell you when we sit at the snack bar.

Jocko minded his manners well enough to pay for her order. He waited for her to gobble down two chocolate-covered donuts before asking again.

Terri answered after draining a large carton of orange juice.

"I'm pregnant, and only you could possibly be the father.

Jocko's mouth opened wide enough to swallow a donut whole, then closed it, saying not a word while scratching his head until Terri caressed his other arm.

"Would you like us to become Co-Friends? If we like it, we can go for a Vow-Cer, complete with a contract and ceremony.

Jocko pulled away before saying,

"I don't know what you're talking about. It sounds too deep for me, at least for now. Neither is having a kid. It'll crimp my style too much. I need time to adjust.

Undeterred, Terri pushed ahead.

"The courts might force you to pay child support even if you don't give a DNA sample for paternity testing."

Jocko's tone became hostile.

"So, you've got it all thought out, huh? You think you've got me by the gonads? What if I pay for an abortion?"

"I'm still thinking about it, but now I know I don't want you to be my co-friend. Goodbye."

Terri held back her tears until reaching home. They poured the moment she found Erika in the kitchen with Cassie at her side starting to make dinner.

Erika said,

"Go play with Lady while I talk to Daddy."

Cassie said nothing while shuffling away. Erika hugged Terri, whispering to herself.

Jocko must have said what she didn't want to hear. I won't say a word until she does.

The deluge subsided enough for Terri to talk.

"He doesn't want a serious relationship and won't lift a finger to help raise a kid.

Slipping her hands to Terri's shoulders, she rocked her gently while saying,

"You must have shocked him to the max. He might change his mind if you give him more time, but you don't need him to have a serious relationship or to help raise a child if you nix the abortion. You've got me.

Terri squeezed tighter for a second before letting go and saying,

"I want to raise a one.

"When did you make that choice?"

"When I saw you and Cassie.

Erika's playful voice would have lifted anyone's mood when she said,

"I'll make something special for supper. What would you like?"

"Anything sweet.

"How about pancakes loaded with butter and maple syrup?"

"You sure you have enough syrup?"

Terri's face looked like the sun had just emerged from behind a cloud when Erika said,

"I always keep an extra bottle. I love pancakes too, almost as much as I love you."

Chapter 18
September 2235

"Who Is the Winner?"

Terri hid her pregnancy by wearing loose-fitting clothes that covered her emergent baby bump while faking her aggressive, high-energy style at the office. But as her fatigue increased, she realized by mid-September she could no longer pretend.

When she told Erika at breakfast, her partner shrugged shoulders and said,

We'll tell Mario this morning. I'm coming with you, and you tell him why we're here."

Sitting in his king-sized chair, Mario pointed to the ladies now sitting in front of his desk when he started talking.

"Well, my dynamic duo comes in. How you coming on the new assignment?"

"That's why we're here. I want to take a pregnancy leave of absence.

Mario leaned as far back as the chair allowed before sputtering.

"You're what? You don't look it.

"Trust me, I am, so here's what you need to do. Promote Erika to fill in while I'm gone. She knows how to do the job.

"Bu-but what are you gonna do?"

"Practice being a mother. I'm going home right now to start."

While Terri told the situation to those in the office, Mario tried to find something to say to Erika, whose insouciant expression unnerved him.

"OK, you can start filling in, but I gotta get Mrs. Harmony's approval to make it official. How you coming on the Project Plan?"

"It's not as good as you need. I won't hit the Halloween deadline unless I hire a research assistant.

"Why don't you use the one that's been working with Terri?"

"My style's different; I must find one who can handle it.

"What the hell's happened to that nice and pleasant Erika?"

"I'm still here, but I'm exercising my situational leadership prerogative. I'll be working at Terri's workstation starting today. You better speak to the troops after Terri goes home. Meanwhile, I'll line up candidates." Erika walked away as Mario's eyes stared at her backside.

After finding a popular job-posting website and downloading its job template, Erika worked for three hours constructing what she would use to find candidates. Then she walked around the office, asking Terri's erstwhile team for their opinions about today's changes announced by Mario.

Only one complained: the researcher whom Mario reassigned to another office. Erika calmed her down by saying,

"When Terri returns, I'm sure she'll ask you to do the same." Then she returned to her workstation, printed two copies of the job description after a final proofreading, and then texted Terri that she would try to be home no later than 8 p.m.

Erika surprised her by coming home at seven. Terri prepared a snack while Erika looked in on Cassie. Erika handed her a copy of the posting when she returned.

Job title:
Entry Level Research Assistant: Offered for a six-month contract. Combination work-at-home and office. Learn on-the-job while utilizing or completing an appropriate college degree.

Our Company:
International Breaking News, an aggressive and proactive provider of investigative stories from around the globe, want you to learn the career of researching a story's background. You will report to a Senior Investigative Reporter at our Manhattan office. Expect a challenging pace that will accelerate your career.

Job Requirements:
- Outstanding writing ability.
- Computer and Internet search skills.
- ChatGPT or equivalent Prompting Experience.
- Demonstrated ability to work under pressure.
- Ability to critique and edit articles and scripts, and then extend content.
- Must be willing to work more than 40 hours per week if deadlines call for it.
- Completed four-year college degree or have it in progress.

Benefits:
- Contract renewal or full-time employment, depending on performance.
- Health, Vision, and Dental plan while working for IBN.
- Competitive Salary.

Contact and Application information:
To be considered, please submit your resume by October 15th to e,kincaid@ibn.com. If it looks promising, we'll contact you to arrange an interview. We look forward reviewing your resume.

To be considered for our summer recruitment round, please submit your application to hr@besttech.com by June 18, 2021. If we accept your application, we'll be in touch to schedule an interview. We look forward to hearing from you.

After skimming it, Terri said,

"Why are you hiring another researcher?"

"I talked with your people after Mario told them what's going on. They're loyal to you, but they've already seen me in action, so I think they'll do a good job for me.

"What about my researcher?"

"I haven't worked with her. I prefer working alone but won't have much time for doing research, and I need someone who can handle my style. And I told her you might bring her back when you return.

"OK, now what happens?"

"I'll post it tomorrow, and when resumes start trickling in, I'll choose five that look good on paper and invite them for a face-to-face interview at the office. Then I make an offer to the one I think will do the best job.

"Wow, you make me proud. You've suddenly become a take-charge person.

Terri saw the twinkle in Erika's eye when she said,

"Mario said sort of the same."

Erika posted the job early the next morning, then worked the rest of the day on the project plan, which she did for the next two days before checking Emails. She stored the resumes that had already come in before re-focusing on the project.

When checking again two days later, a flood of over one hundred resumes had inundated her Email inbox. She stored them and suspended the job posting to stop the deluge. After that, she walked to the vending machine for a Coca-Cola. She returned to her workstation and mused while sipping.

How am I going to wade through all the resumes? Hey, I'll use a Chat-GPT online resume-screening app. Once I describe what I want in the prompt box, the software finds the top candidates. Then I print them out and bring the candidates in. Five should be plenty.

Printing them an hour later, Erika studied each resume to prepare for the in-person interviews. After spending three hours making notes, she was about to close the office when revelations emerged.

I was so busy looking at each resume's details I didn't notice the distribution – two males and three females. It's fitting too, because that ratio mirrors the national average.

And I just realized that neither job postings nor resumes list age or racial backgrounds for fear of discrimination. I can figure that out when I see them, but I can get a head start by surfing the web. Let's see what I get.

Erika had the information an hour later.

The ages are close together, which is to be expected because they're undergrads, but look at the racial mix – one White male, two Black females, one Latino female, and one Chinese male. I think it shows that college admissions discriminated by race are now in the past tense.

Erika sent EMails, giving an interview date and time instead of asking when they would like to be interviewed. She planned to interview one each day the following week.

After all the candidates came and went, Erika reviewed her notes and selected the one she liked the best.

I wish I could hire them all, but that's not the way the corporate world works, so I'll select the one that's slightly above the rest: one of the Black females.

Erika sent an Email to the winning candidate, telling her to come to the office tomorrow at 8 a.m., even though it would be Saturday. She also sent diplomatically-worded rejection letters to the others.

Erika arrived at 7:30 on the interview day, bringing a mood-elevating selection of donuts, muffins, and soft drinks she set in the break room before starting the coffee maker. When two team members came in soon after, she asked why they were working this Saturday. After they told her, she gave them suggestions. They were about to walk away when she explained who would arrive at eight and how they could help with the interview.

The candidate arrived at 7:50. Erika made her wait fifteen minutes before taking her to the break room. Then they went to a cubicle where Erika dived into the interview.

"You have to answer these questions – what's your biggest weakness, where do you want to be in five years, and why should I hire you?"

The candidate, a Black female pursuing an undergraduate liberal arts degree while working online part-time doing information searches for the public library, answered all questions succinctly.

Then Erika asked,

"Before I let you go, what's your favorite book that articulates the commonsense rules for writing?"

"Why, it's 'The Elements of Style,' by Strunk and White.

"Excellent choice, and now I'll tell you what I'm –" the two team members rushed into her office and interrupted her words.

The candidate slid out of the way. The team fellow who barged in first screamed,

"This deadline is impossible. You're pushing too hard.

Erika said,

"Calm down. We'll figure this out after I say goodbye to the person I'm interviewing.

The teamers left, the candidate sat, and Erika said,

"Where were we?"

"I think you were about to say 'I'll tell you what I'm about to do.' Is that correct?"

"Yes, here's what it is – I am hiring you. Do you want the job?"

"I'd love to work for you.

"Excellent choice, and by the way, everyone here is nicer than what you saw. We planned the pushy questions and office argument as your final exam. You did great.

"When do I start?"

"As soon as you're ready.

"I'm ready now.

"How does a week from Monday sound?"

"I like the sound and won't let you down."

Chapter 19
October 2235

"Blowing in the Wind"

Erika had seen Electra's wisdom emerge ever since coming under her tutelage. Whenever she compared the outcomes from her life-changing events to what Electra said, pieces of her mystical guidance would burst to life. That was just one of the reasons she invoked Electra's avatar several times a week.

She was now listening at midnight on October's fourth Friday to Electra summarize her happy situation.

"Indeed, much has turned in your favor –Terri's decision to have a child, your promotion, and the young researcher you hired. Even the title of your next project sounds promising.

Erika positively glowed from the compliment.

"I know Mario will like 'Terrorists' Potential Means for Launching Surprise Attacks'. I'll give him several copies next Monday, and I plan to keep everything moving in the right direction.

"I commend your determination, but remember this –

mere mortals have only limited control of outcomes. Try as they might, unforeseen events might leave them like a leaf blowing in the wind. You must always stay alert and have options.

"Thanks for the advice. I'll let you know in a couple of days what's been happening.

Electra disappeared faster than the fading light when Erika turned off the lamp and headed for bed.

Erika luxuriated the entire day, enjoying the tranquility of the moment and dividing time between watching Cassie and chatting with Terri. While watching Cassie and Lady lounge around that evening, Terri said,

"I've got a craving for chocolate ice cream. Would you please go get some?"

"Sure, I'm in the mood for some too. The weather's still pleasant, so I'll take Cassie while Lady keeps you company. We'll be back soon."

Erika loaded the stroller with what she always kept close, then strapped Cassie in and moved out.

The light breeze and full moon added to the joy she had felt the entire day. The half-hour stroll seemed like only a moment. She picked up the pace when exiting the supermarket to keep the ice cream from softening too much, but not by much.

Nothing disturbed the surroundings until she heard distant sirens that grew louder as she approached her apartment building. When the sounds stopped, she made guesses.

Those could be from a squad car, an ambulance, or maybe a fire truck. Whatever it is, I hope no one's in too much danger or pain.

She had walked another block when a tremendous explosion coming from the direction of her building ripped the air.

She pushed as hard as she could without upsetting Cassie.

Ten minutes later, she saw an emerging catastrophe: an explosion in her apartment building. Flames leaped from windows on her apartment's floor. She and the firefighters could only stand and gape until piecing together a plan of action.

A growing crowd stood with her, watching as the firefighters rushed in to rescue people near the blown-up apartment. Erika's panic rose close to the screaming point as hoses and police tried to control the fire and surroundings. Thirty minutes later, they did.

Erika moved closer to the fire chief, listening to what he was saying to the police commander. A reporter from the first news truck that had just arrived also listened.

"Somebody might have left a gas stove on but forgot to light it until it was too late."

The commander asked,

"Could it be a bombing?"

"We can't tell until we go in, But one thing's certain – no one survived."

The reporter asked,

"Do you know who lives in that apartment?"

"One of the persons we rescued said a Ms. Marilyn Tarrant and Erika Kincaid, but she didn't know if they and their little girl got out.

Erika was about to barge in when her brain elevated to the take-action state. She started pushing as hard as she could to a near-by place where she could figure out what to do.

She pulled her cell phone from the bag and called Ava while on the move. When she answered, Erika's tense words took over.

"I need to come over ASAP. I'm about ten minutes away with Cassie in the stroller. Please meet me in the lobby.

"We'll be there.

Halting in front of Ava, Erika's words rushed out.

"There was an accident at the apartment. Cassie and I were out but Terri was there when an explosion and fire destroyed the place. I don't know Terri's status, and I need you to take care of Cassie until I find out. Take the stroller to your apartment, put Cassie to bed, and the ice cream in the fridge.

Erika grabbed her bag before Ava said,

"What about Lady? Did she escape?"

"She might have. Dogs have survival instincts that often work better than ours. If there's no trace in the rubble, there's a possibility she's show up on her own.

Seeing Erika's agitation, Ava ended her part of the conversation by saying,

"Please let us know how Terri is," before she wheeled the stroller and followed Ivana to the elevator.

Erika sat for a minute on a sofa in the lobby, calming herself before calling Electra and speaking immediately when the avatar appeared.

"I need your help. Our apartment blew up with Terri in it and I don't know if she survived. Is there something you can do to find her?"

"If her cell phone is still working or she has an embedded tracking chip, I can run my Object Locator app. What might have caused it?"

"My worst fear is kidnappers who covered their tracks by using a bomb. What can you do if that's the case?"

A never-seen-before GUI scrolled on the screen while Electra explained.

Terminator Weapon App
Input: Big Data
Target
Prompt of My Choosing (Who What Why
Where When How)

Output
Location:
City/State/Address GPS Position
Status:
Resolution Outcome
Accuracy (Percent)

"I will run my Terminator Weapon to eliminate the threat.

"Doing all this is gonna take even you more time than I've got. While you're doing what you can, I'll call another person who said awhile ago he'd help if I needed it.

Electra vanished. No words were needed.

Erika sat perfectly still, trying to recall the phone number of the only person left. All at once, it flashed into her consciousness as it emerged from memory. She steeled her nerves, took a deep breath, and dialed. Her spirits soared when she recognized the voice.

"You called. Whatcha want?"

"Vincenzo, it's Erika Kincaid. I need your help."

"Where are ya?"

"With some friends.

"Gimme da address, then go stand outside. I'll come getcha.

"How soon?"

"As fast as my best driver moves.

Vincenzo disconnected as soon as she told him.

Erika settled down enough to offer a tiny prayer to whatever gods might control the constantly emerging Universe. Then she ran to the rendezvous.

Fifteen minutes later, a dark sedan with tinted windows rumbled to a stop in front of the entrance. When the rear door on her side opened, a gritty voice yelled,

"Get in." She recognized Vincenzo's voice and did so with two lightning-quick steps. Then he yelled, "Take us to da usual place."

The car sped silently away.

He turned on the back seat interior lights before turning toward Erika and then asking,

"What's da story?"

Some bad people blew up my apartment two hours ago, and my partner was in it. They might have kidnapped her and used a bomb to cover their tracks.

"Who d'ya think is after her?"

"Government agencies or their Big-Business cronies who don't like our news videos telling people the truth. Or it could be an international conspiracy of countries that don't like us.

"What d'ya want me ta do?"

"Your people know what's going on. Maybe they heard something about some sort of contract on her, me, or both to do something that'll shut us up.

Vincenzo spoke immediately.

"Lieutenants and enforcers are wait'en for us. Save your words til we get there.

"OK. I have some, but I hope theirs are better than mine.

Vincenzo doused the lights and made one call before settling back. Erika leaned back to rest, but the situation changed when the driver's terse words broke the silence.

"Flashing lights turned on behind."
Vincenzo issued an equally terse command.
"Make'em disappear.
"Will do. Buckle up."

Chapter 20
October 2235

"The Termination Gang"

The car blasted forward, pinning Erika to the seat and blurring her view through the side window. Then the driver slammed the brakes, skidded around a corner, and rocketed away.

He repeated the maneuver until no sirens remained, then drove at normal speed until turning into a dark alley and pulling into what might be a warehouse. The driver opened Vincenzo's door and motioned for Erika to follow.

When the driver flipped a light switch, Erika saw they were in a loading dock that held two black SUVs with tinted windows. They followed him to a side door that he opened and then stood aside. Vincenzo entered first with Erika right behind.

They entered a barren room holding three tables strung together holding twelve tough-looking enforcers and two chairs in front. Vincenzo signaled for everyone to sit before following suit and then speaking.

"Erika Kincaid's got a problem and needs our help. Listen to her. Capiche?"

"Only affirmative nods answered.

He pointed to Erika, who told everything she knew. One enforcer spoke when she finished.

"We already checked our sources. They say The Termination Gang took someone to headquarters, and it could be her partner.

There ain't no love lost between us and them. We gotta break in to know for sure.

Vincenzo gave the orders.

"Here's da drill. Six plus Erika and Doc take one SUV. Da rest stay here. Da driver gets-em to da place and da lieutenant and two enforcer pairs get set. Driver stays put. It'll be lights' out, so put on night-vision goggles. Da explosives handler blows da door. Da lead pair storms in using two-by-two dynamic cover entry. Da other follows, and Erika trails. Rub out all gang members; den Doc goes in, den all come back. Questions?"

When only silence answered, Vincenzo issued the last command. "Go."

The driver kept headlights on until approaching the termination gang's headquarters. Then he parked out of sight of any posted guard, and the enforcers moved into position. Everyone stood back while the handler prepared for detonation.

KABOOM. They charged in after enough smoke and debris cleared. Diving to the floor, Erika couldn't see the action, but she heard deadly-sounding RAT-A-TAT-TATS. She stayed prone until the gunfire stopped and the lights came on.

The enforcers searched for Terri, and Erika joined for identification. She could feel her pounding pulse, and when she heard a voice yell,

"She's here," it pounded even harder. She raced to the spot just in time to see two enforcers helping Terri stand.

Hugging her, Erika took their place and then made a quick inspection.

"I don't see any injuries. Do you feel good enough to—" One of the men yelled,

"Hold the reunion later. We gotta go before the cops get here.

With Erika's arms locked around Terri, two enforcers put the girls in the SUV, and it sped away seconds later.

The adrenaline level kept everyone's nerves wired for action and words bottled up. Erika's arms still enfolded her partner, and she had a clear view out the side window because she was sitting next to the door. She whispered,

"We'll soon be in a safe place, and tomorrow we'll –" The SUV's sudden swerve to the left cut off her words. Flashing blue lights and a hail of bullets told why.

The men in the third row shot out the back window and began returning fire at the squad on their tail, but another rammed them from the side opposite Erika, launching the SUV into an out-of-control spin. Erika's brain elevated to its highest state when she heard bullets raking close to the gas tank. As the spin slowed and the gas tank erupted, Erika pushed the door open and pulled herself and Terri out just before she hit her head on the pavement.

She still had one arm locked on Terri when she came to. She saw the SUV ablaze but far enough ahead to keep them away from the flames. The police hadn't spotted them yet, but Erika's blood ran cold when she looked at Terri.

Gasping for breath, Terri lay in a pool of blood. Erika stroked her face while kneeling close.

"Please don't move until I check your injuries, OK?"

Terri stuttered,

"Oh-oh, Erika. I-I wanted us to be a fa-family of four, but it's not in the-the—" before her words trailed away.

Erika listened for a pulse, then checked her breathing before pounding on her chest to bring life back, but after fifteen minutes, she knew.

There's nothing else I can do. She's gone.

Erika's screams followed by tears pierced the darkness. She covered her face to hide sobs that lasted until a sudden resolve washed over her.

She pulled herself up after giving Terri a lingering kiss that etched a timeless image before saying a final prayer that emerged from memory.

Farewell, my love – my Special One,
I tried my best but failed.
I grieve My Loss – but for how long?
Unknown – My Spirit has been Impaled.

But this I know – what you Command,
Leads to an Emergent Trail.
From where I find our Singular Place,
In a Future where we Prevail.

Part of You is part of Me,
Forever it will always Be.

THE END